Summer
at
Bramblewood
Farm

A gorgeous summer romance guaranteed to pull the heart strings

Abby Broomfield

FIRST EDITION

abbybroomfieldauthor@hotmail.com

About the Author

Abby Broomfield was born and raised on her family farm on the Isle of Wight. She can often be found down in the horse field reading, up by the pig pen writing, or among the cows, daydreaming.

With a background in child education, her aspirations to become a primary school teacher soon switched to following her dream and becoming an author. She couldn't think of a better way to spend her life than enriching it with words and imagination. She took the plunge and now presents you with Summer at Bramblewood Farm, the first of many books to come.

Abby loves to hear from her readers and if you'd like to get in touch then please go ahead and contact her using any of the options below.

Email: abbybroomfieldauthor@hotmail.com

Instagram: @abbybroomfieldauthor

Facebook: Abby Broomfield Author

Twitter: @ASBroomfield1

Rome

Rome Buckley watched the watery sunlight rise above the trees at the far end of the valley. He had been up since the early hours, feeding and bedding up his two hundred head of young cattle. Now, he was on his way to check the ewes. Another few weeks and they would start to give birth. Worry washed over him at the thought of lambing three hundred and fifty sheep by himself. He just couldn't fathom how he would manage. Why did Seth have to break his leg at one of their busiest times of the year? Rome would just have to stick him out in the barn on a chair to keep watch over the flock while he took breaks to sleep. Damn sheep, always giving birth in the middle of the night.

He picked his way along the stream that cut through the middle of the lower paddock and ran out into the creek, stepping over the rocks and through the ankle deep water. The sheep were grazing over at the far side, down by the marshes. The sun peeked higher as he strode across the field and the fresh feeling of spring encircled him. He felt tension leaving his shoulders as he gazed across the familiar view. Even though this morning promised good weather, he knew he'd have to move the sheep into the barn while they gave birth. That way he could keep a close eye on them and the lambs wouldn't have to face the wet nights ahead. He would lamb them in the safety of the barn and turn them out once they were strong enough. Another job added to the list: getting that barn ready for lambing.

As Rome reached the ewes, he cast his eyes over the flock looking for any that might be in trouble. He saw one had managed to get tangled in the hedgerow at the back of the flock. They parted as he moved through them and made his way towards the distressed sheep. It wriggled and tried to break free as he approached, but Rome reached the animal and put an arm around its neck to steady it. He covered his hand with the sleeve of his wax jacket and picked away at the brambles. He let go and, with one last pull, the sheep freed itself and bolted back to the others.

Rome gazed over the stock fence at the creek as a gaggle of Canadian geese flew down and settled on the surface of the water. The tide was out and he watched some moorhens run across the mud flats to hide in the reedy grass. He directed his attention back to the sheep and decided he was going to have to find some help until Seth's leg was better. Rome trudged his way back up the valley, whistling to his collie dogs, Tess and Birdie, who darted from the thorny hedgerow and bounded after him.

Rome reached the gate to the farmhouse and made his way inside. He took off his wet boots in the outhouse and hung his jacket by the sink. He went inside, two dogs in tow, and flipped the kettle on. He was wondering where he could find a farm hand as he took down a mug and filled it with a heaped teaspoon of coffee and two sugars. Turning and leaning against the sink, his hands gripped the sideboard and his head hung low as he thought. Maybe he could drive into the village and ask Doris if he could put a sign in the window of the newsagents. But then, what good would that do? He knew everyone in the small village and they all had jobs. Perhaps he could go to the library and get one of them to help him put an advertisement online. That was what he'd have to do; he'd drink this coffee then head down to the library. He glanced at the clock. 6:30 AM. He'd have to wait a few hours until it was open.

*

A few hours later a bell tinkled as Rome ducked through the doorway of the little stone library. He wanted to get it done quickly. He didn't have time to be going out like this when he had so many things to do on the farm. A niggling anxiety gnawed at him; all he wanted to do was get back to the farm and work.

Mandy Smith smiled at him as he made his way over to the post office counter.

"Rome! Fancy seeing you here. What can I help you with?" Mandy leapt up and flounced around the side of the counter, then leant back on her hands, exposing the flesh scarcely hidden by her obscenely low cut blouse. Rome forced himself to smile, when in truth, Mandy got on his nerves,

"I need to put an advertisement online, Mandy. I need a farm hand. Seth has broken his leg and it's almost lambing season," he explained.

Mandy smiled.

"I could help you up at the farm on my days off," she suggested, moving towards him.

Rome glanced down at her long hot pink nails and black stilettos. "It's kind of you, Mandy, but I need a man."

He cleared his throat and averted his gaze. He just wanted to get this over and done with so he could get back to clearing his lambing shed.

"You know, that's quite sexist Rome. I'm actually very strong and I don't mind getting dirty, you know?" Mandy twirled a piece of hair around her finger as a smile spread across her face. Rome wondered what Georgina would think of her flirtatiousness, but the thought left him seconds after it had arrived.

"What would the post office and library do without you? Now, can you show me this computer?" Rome smiled for Mandy's benefit, but sighed inwardly as he rubbed his chin. She led Rome to the far side of the little library, to a spot behind a stack of books where a little computer sat with a massive box attached to the back.

"Don't you have a phone? You know? Like a Facebook account you could post on?" Mandy leant over to turn on the computer almost exposing the bottom of her bum cheeks beneath her mini skirt.

"Yes I have a phone, Mandy," said Rome, adjusting his gaze and shuffling to one side. "But it just does the basics, calling and texting. No Facebook."

"Why don't you get one? Then you can send pictures and stuff." Mandy tilted her head up, revealing a smirk.

In Rome's twenty eight years, he had never needed or wanted a smart phone and he was certain it would stay that way. He had certainly never sent pictures to anyone.

"We don't really get much signal on the farm. Anyway, how about I get you to do me a massive favour," he began, trying to speed this interaction along. "If I write down what I want the advertisement to say then maybe you can post it to a couple of places for me and put my number in there?"

Mandy went to retrieve a pen and some paper, which she thrust into Rome's grasp, grazing the backs of his hands with her false nails. Rome smiled awkwardly, took the paper and put it down on the little computer table, where he began to scribble out the essentials of what he would need from a farm hand. *Immediate start, strong, hard working. Accommodation available on the farm.* He handed the paper to Mandy, who batted her long eyelashes as she glanced down at it.

"Oh, you forgot your number." Mandy handed the paper back to Rome, who took out his little phone and flipped up the screen. Some dust and hay fell out, drifting to the floor. Rome saw Mandy glance down but she didn't comment.

"How do I find my number?" he asked, praying this could be over soon. Mandy giggled as she reached out her hand.

"I'll show you," she said, plucking the phone from Rome's grasp. He didn't know how she would manage to press the buttons with those ridiculous nails. He struggled enough having big hands. He was always clicking two buttons at once. Somehow, though, Mandy managed it quickly and leant across Rome to take the paper back, jotting down his number on the table. He hoped for his sake she wouldn't save it in her phone. He would keep it turned off if that was the case. The last thing he needed was women harassing him, whether it was flattering or not.

"I'll get to work now and I'm sure you'll get a call, Rome." Mandy's lips curved into a smile as she leant back against the little computer table, accentuating her open blouse.

"Great, thanks for your help." Rome bolted for the door, escaping back out into the fresh, cool air. Flipping the collar of his jacket up he headed straight for his Landrover. Although spring was here and summer approaching, the cold was still lingering in the air. He hopped into his Landrover, where Tess and Birdie sprung up from the back seats, wagging and licking.

"Lie down. Good girls." Rome plunged the Landrover into gear and drove off past the library where he saw Mandy wave to him through the window. Pretending not to see, he aimed his gaze forwards and drove on. Rome drove past the newsagents, past the little primary school, past the church and out of Addleton down narrow country lanes on his way back to Bramblewood Farm. There were no houses for miles, just countryside, rolling hills and the patchwork fields of South Devon which stretched for miles. The marshlands and the creek led out into the sea, both fed by small tributaries of fresh water from higher up in the valleys.

Rome reached the farm, let the dogs out and made his way over to the barn to begin the big job of clearing it out. There was machinery that needed to be moved elsewhere and hurdles that needed to be set up because each individual ewe would have its own pen until their lamb was a few days old. As they all made it through the first month or so of spring he could turn them back out into the valley. Rome slipped off his jacket which he tossed over a gate and then set to work.

*

The next morning, after Rome had finished tending to the animals, he sat at the kitchen table with a cup of coffee as he leafed through his *Farmers' Weekly*. He was startled from his thoughts as his phone sprang to life in his pocket. He dug it out and stared, momentarily perplexed, at the small screen. He never got calls, not unless it was Georgina yapping his ear off, but he didn't recognise the number on the screen. It finally hit him that it was probably a call about his advert for a farm hand.

"Hello?" he answered eagerly.

"Hi Rome, it's Mandy." Oh good lord, he knew he shouldn't have exposed his phone number like that.

"Mandy. What's up?" he said, in a monotone of annoyance.

"I took the liberty of putting the library number down for your advert so I could filter potential farm hands because I know how busy you are. And I found one. They can meet you at the farm at lunchtime if that suits?"

Mandy seemed pleased with herself. Rome knew he should be grateful even though he was perfectly aware Mandy was doing this to get in his pants, not to help him out. His heart did lift at the news, though. He might have someone to help him and Seth out after all. Seth would be pleased as well.

"Great Mandy. I appreciate it. Is that all?" Rome asked hurriedly. "It's just I'm trying to tackle an awkward cow." He made a grunting noise as he lied.

"Oh sure," she chimed. "Don't be a stranger, Rome. Remember you have my number now; you can save it," she added with her trademark flirtatious giggle.

"Sure, see you Mandy." Rome hung up and put his coffee down on the wooden kitchen table. He ran his hands through his dark curls and rested his head in his palms for a while. He breathed a sigh of relief. Now all he could do was wait and hope this person would be up to the job. He should have asked for a name. There was no way in hell he'd ring Mandy back, though. He couldn't be bothered with that. He'd just have to wait and see who turned up tomorrow.

Emily

Emily Rogers carefully drove her black BMW down the narrow country lane, praying she wouldn't meet a tractor. Her new car had been shiny and clean when she had left the outskirts of London but now it was splattered with mud and shrouded in dust. She winced and clutched the steering wheel as she hit a pothole. With gritted teeth and a firm hold on the wheel she steered around a few more. The car crawled up the road, which was lined with a fluffy canopy of oaks. The setting sun flicked in and out of her vision as it glinted between the trunks of the trees as she continued down the road.

The instructions hadn't been clear on where the turning to the farm was. All she knew was that it was out in the middle of nowhere, but she would find it if she just kept driving. Apparently, if she reached the beach she had gone too far. The satnav had only gotten her so far before it began to get confused on the spider web network of farm tracks. She was looking for a sign for Bramblewood Farm. Finally, she saw a wooden gate in the distance. She scanned desperately for a sign. Failing to see one, she stopped the car and wrenched the handbrake up with a little sigh.

Emily got out of the car and her heel sunk straight down into the mud on the verge side. She looked upward with closed eyes and let out a long breath. She instantly regretted wearing her favourite black heels. Feeling exasperated, Emily pulled her foot out of the mud and set it down tentatively onto the rough road. She wobbled over to the wooden gate and peered around. A long track swerved into the distance, with grass growing up the middle in a strip and deep tire marks rutting either side. *Please*, she thought, *don't let this be it*. Then the sign caught her eye, buried deep in the hedge and engulfed in years of overgrown blackthorn.

Welcome to Bramblewood Farm.

Beginning to feel annoyed by this whole situation Emily started to wonder why she had let her boss bully her into doing this evaluation. It was miles from London, where she lived and worked. It had taken her hours to get here. Devon was a trek, and her boss knew she didn't like driving. She felt flustered and clammy from sitting in the car. All she wanted to do right then was go back to her apartment, shower and watch *Selling Sunset* on Netflix as she sipped red wine. She knew nothing about farms and not much about their worth. She certainly didn't know why her boss had picked her for the job, other than that the woman who dealt with the rural properties was on maternity leave and apparently there was no one more suitable for the job than Emily. She highly doubted that as she pondered her boss's ulterior motives for sending her away. She tried to look on the bright side. It would be another arrow in her quiver. After valuing the farm she would be able to add that to her list of skills, not that a knowledge of farm prices would do her much good in London.

Finding the latch to the wooden gate she swung it open then got back into her car. She pulled a tissue from her handbag and attempted to wipe the heel of her shoe. Pressing her foot down on the pedal she inched down the track. After a few metres there was a grinding noise and a jiggling vibration under her feet. *Oh God.* She slowly pulled forward but it ground louder and something came free with a loud snapping noise. She sucked in air through her teeth as her car stalled and came to a jerking halt. That wasn't good.

Burning with annoyance, she swung the car door open and checked the ground for mud before putting her feet down. She tried to lean forward to see under the car, but couldn't see well enough. Taking a deep breath she got down on her hands and knees. Great, something was definitely hanging loose from the bottom. Perfect. Emily stood up and brushed off her knees, thinking about how the gorgeous, successful women from her favourite series, *Selling Sunset,* would never have to deal with situations like this. She looked down the long farm track and sighed as she reached into the car to get her handbag. She had to get there, one way or another.

Emily took out her keys and locked her car. She slung them into her handbag as she began to walk precariously down the rutty farm track. She walked down the tree lined lane until she came to an opening. By the light from the setting sun she could make out the outline of a house and open fields stretching all around. The visibility was bad and she struggled to see. A sudden thought of who would fix her car crossed her mind, and she continued on until she reached the farmyard.

A huge barn loomed ahead. She could hear what she could only assume to be cows in there shuffling around and mooing. Her brow furrowed at the thought of the scary, huge beasts. Emily crossed the yard and made her way towards the house, through a little garden gate and down the path. That's when her shoe slipped on the smooth, worn down cobbles and she lost her balance. Falling gracelessly to the ground she hit her bum and elbow hard on the floor. Her handbag and its contents scattered across the path.

She cursed and groaned, utterly embarrassed at how this was turning out but grateful no one had seen her. How unprofessional. This really wasn't her day.

To her sheer mortification she heard heavy footsteps in the yard behind her.

"Are you okay?" a deep voice asked. Emily brushed the blond hair from her face, which had fallen loose from her neat bun, and tried to stand. She got half way to her feet as a large hand reached out and helped her up. She turned and to her despair saw the man holding her hand was a tall, dark haired, handsome one. His attractiveness made her heart pick up its pace but only because of increased feelings of embarrassment. Had he been an old, ugly farmer, Emily would have been able to cope with the fact that she had fallen flat on her face in front anther human. Even in the dimming light she could see his eyes were bright blue. His hair was messy but charming, curling at his forehead. Emily felt her backside throb from the fall and was distracted by a sharp pain in her elbow. The man slipped his hand out of hers and she was further embarrassed to realise she had been holding it this entire time in awkward silence. The man looked her up and down slowly. He had a strange expression, confusion maybe. He certainly didn't look pleased.

"Sorry," Emily blurted out. "How awfully embarrassing." She quickly bent to collect her handbag and started filling it with the scattered items: lipstick, her phone, her purse and oh God, a box of tampons. Emily felt her face glow with heat. She cleared her throat and a little squeak escaped. She straightened herself and smoothed her hands down over her slim frame to correct her outfit. Emily wasn't sure if she was going to laugh or burst into tears. The man's gaze remained heavily upon her. He stood a head taller than her and continued to eye her before saying, simply but rudely:

"You're late. And you're a lass. I asked for a man."

Emily picked up an Irish accent, although it wasn't overly pronounced. What did he mean he wanted a man? Since when did people start becoming fussy over the gender of their estate agent?

"I know, I know it's so unprofessional of me. My car, you see, it got stuck in your track and..." Emily stumbled over her words as she tried to apologise for her lateness.

Just then, the man swivelled round and looked out into the yard. Emily followed his gaze.

He cursed and it came out in a growl.

She could make out large shapes moving fast towards where she'd just come from, down the farm track.

"The cows are out! Quick, we can outrun them; you circle right and I'll go left and we can head them off before they get all the way down the track." The man whistled and two dogs appeared by his side. He whistled some more and called some words and the dogs shot off after the huge, black beasts.

Emily stood, frozen mouth agape as the man darted out of the gate and ran left out round the treeline, apparently to cut off the cows. Emily looked down at her heels, then in a split second decision trotted off after them. She went right and tried to go as fast as she could after the animals, only to realise that on the other side of the tree line the space off the track was a grassy field, wet with mud. Emily's shoes sank down into the mud and she felt the cold liquid squelch in between her toes, filling up her heels. She flung her arms up, grimacing, and pulled her feet out of the mud. Step by step, she tried to squelch her away across the field and down the treeline. She felt as though she were in a horror movie, trying to catch her worst fear, covered with mud. She'd break an ankle at this rate.

As she reached the halfway point of the track she heard heavy footsteps coming towards her. It was the farmer. She stopped as he ran past her and back down into the yard. Then she heard the revving of an engine. The farmer pulled up in his Landrover next to her and shouted at her to get in. Emily pulled her feet from the mud with a squelch and made her way through the trees. She clambered into the passenger side of the beaten up vehicle.

She breathed deeply in and out, trying to get her breath back. The Landrover carried the faint smell of oil and something else Emily couldn't detect. The thought of coming face to face with a cow was too much to bear and, on top of that, her favourite shoes would have to be thrown away. She desperately tugged at her seatbelt as the man sped down the track. They hit pot holes so hard she flew off the seat, landing heavily back down on her bruised bum. She winced as her elbow knocked the door.

"Some bright spark left the gate open and now I've got three cows out on the loose," the man grunted. Emily felt her face burnt with embarrassment.

"I'm so sorry. I didn't realise it had to be shut. I feel terrible."

"Number one rule on the farm, leave gates the way you found them." The man kept his eyes directed forward as he hurtled down the track, but she could see his jaw clenched in anger and a muscle twitching at his temple. Emily jumped as she felt something wet on the back of her neck. She whirled her head round to see the dogs, their tails wagging furiously at her. She grimaced as their wet tongues slobbered her face.

"I don't really know a lot about farms," Emily tried to explain. The man abruptly cut her off, seeming not to hear her.

"Trust Mandy to find someone like you. I shouldn't have bothered going to the library," the man huffed.

"Who's–" Emily was cut off as the man abruptly stopped the car on the road and jumped out. Her hand rested on the dashboard to steady herself. He let his dogs out and shouted some commands and they turned the cows in the road and sent them heading back towards the track.

"Get out and stand up the road. Shoo them down the track. Don't let them past you or they'll end up on the beach," the man shouted.

Emily was aghast. She was terrified of cows. She scrambled out of the Landrover and stumbled out into the road. Her legs turned into a wobbling mess as the cows ran towards her.

"Wave your arms," the man ordered from the opposite side of the road. Emily waved her arms erratically and then squealed and hunched up. The animals turned just before they reached her and ran down the track. Her heart hammered in her chest. The man bundled his way back into the Landrover and the dogs jumped in through an open window. Emily stood frozen for a moment before getting back in at the man's hasty request. They sped off down the track, went out round Emily's abandoned car and drove after the cows.

They reached the farmyard and the man ushered the animals back into their barn, then tied the gate up. He walked up and down the front of the barn looking at the gates and then came to an open one which had been pushed ajar. He picked up a frayed piece of orange string from the ground.

"Bastards chewed their way out," he looked up at Emily, half cracking a smile. She didn't smile back.

The last thing she felt like doing was smiling. She was trying to process what had just happened in the space of the last twenty minutes. Maybe she was in shock. The farmer retied the gate then ran his hands through his hair as he breathed a deep sigh. Once again the man looked her up and down, a smile playing on his lips.

"Don't you think wellies would have been more suitable? Maybe a coat? A shirt rather than a silk blouse?" He seemed to find it funny judging by the way his eyes sparkled.

"What's so funny?" Emily snapped. "I was almost trampled and all you care about is my choice of shoes!" The man regarded her, amused.

"So, how many farms have you worked on before?" he asked, pulling up his jeans and holding his belt buckle as he watched her. Emily was confused.

"I haven't really valued many farms. The woman from our country department is on maternity leave and so I've filled in. I do apartments in London, I never normally come this far out into the countryside, that's her job, but–"

"Excuse me?" The man's expression creased into one of confusion as he cut Emily off, silencing her nervous ramble. "Are you saying you're not here to work on the farm?"

Emily frowned.

"I'm here to value your property. This is Bramblewood Farm, correct? You're Mr Buckley?"

Emily asked. The man was silent for a long time. Emily started to wonder if he had heard. "Mr Buckley?"

"I never asked for my property to be valued." He scowled.

"I got sent by my boss to value a Bramblewood Farm belonging to Mr Buckley. Has there been some sort of mix up?"

"You've wasted your time. Go home." The man grunted and turned to walk away.

"Wait," Emily spluttered. The man stopped but didn't turn around. She looked down at her mud drenched feet, her torn silk blouse, her laddered tights. She brushed loose blond hair from her face. She felt her elbow throbbing. Tears brimmed in her eyes, and she tried to hold them back. How ridiculous, why would she cry now? She cleared her throat and swiped the tears from her eyes.

"My car is broken, and I don't know how I'll get home. I came all the way from London." Emily swallowed. The man turned to look at her. She couldn't read his expression. He sighed audibly as he faced her.

"Well, what's wrong with it?" he asked, impatience evident in his brisk and unfriendly tone.

"I don't know," she admitted. "A part has fallen off the bottom and it's stuck."

The man was silent for a few more seconds.

"I'll have a look at it when I go and shut the gate. Give me the keys."

Emily handed them over and he turned and began to walk towards his Landrover, then paused.

"You can wait in the house if you like. It's not locked. Get yourself a cup of tea or something." The man flung out his hand, indicating the house and then disappeared down the track. Emily stood silent for a moment, listening to his engine rumble down the track before rushing inside. She was cold and covered with mud, she could murder a cup of tea.

She pushed open the door to the big stone farmhouse. She found a light switch and flicked it on, revealing a little stone entry room. The floor was flagstone, with wooden doors to the right and to the left. Emily went right and it brought her to the kitchen. She made a beeline for the kettle and noticed her hand was shaking as she reached to flip it on. She was used to making herself at home in other people's houses. She did it often enough when she valued properties and took people on viewings. Still, this man seemed to dislike her, which made it more awkward to be making tea in his kitchen. She found a mug and filled it with two sugars and a tea bag and looked down at her feet, her heels were dripping in mud and she had walked it across the man's floors. Annoyed and embarrassed she left the kitchen to remove them. She went back out through the door, passed the entryway and into the outhouse. She removed her shoes and placed them up on the draining board by the sink. Her tights were torn and splattered with mud up to the bottom of her calves. She looked up at the front door and then reached her skirt up to pull her tights down. She peeled them off and bundled them onto her ruined shoes. Her skin was stained brown but at least the mud wasn't dripping off of her.

She imagined what her boss would think of her if he could see her now. After he heard of this, Emily was certain that he would choose Sophie for the upcoming promotion instead of her. Perfect Sophie, on whom her boss definitely had his eye.

Emily tiptoed back to the kitchen and poured hot water into her mug, then walked to the fridge to find some milk. There wasn't much in there. Some meat, milk and ketchup. By that she guessed that the farmer lived alone. She held the warm mug of tea in her shaking hands and closed her eyes, breathing deeply.

The back door opened. Emily straightened up and cleared her throat as the farmer strode into the kitchen in his dirty work boots. The farmer stood before her with large hands on his hips. He gazed at her bare, muddy legs. She was hardly embarrassed considering the rest of tonight's mishaps.

"Your car is beyond buggered, to put it mildly, miss. I'll call a mechanic in the morning." His expression bore a strange darkness which put Emily on edge. The man wandered over to the kitchen table which he leant against, eyes still lingering on Emily.

"Thank you. Do you know a place I could sleep tonight? Are there any hotels around here? I was supposed to stay in one an hour's drive away from here but I can't drive there now. Maybe you have a local taxi number I could call?" Emily pressed the mug of warm tea to her lips and sipped as she watched the farmer consider her question.

"No, this is a small village, there's a little B&B but it's too late to knock on their door. There's no taxi services around here; you'd have to call one from further away. You may as well just stay here. What's the point in faffing around?"

He didn't sound happy about it and the offer made Emily's heart race. Surely it wasn't safe to stay with a stranger. She didn't even know his first name. But as she quickly considered her options there didn't seem to be many. Calling a taxi meant waiting hours for it to get here. They were deep in the middle of nowhere and then it meant hours of driving in the dark back to the city. Her car was broken, so it would make sense to stay until it was fixed. There was no other easy way home.

"I don't want to be a burden," Emily said at last.

The farmer shrugged. "It's a big house, it won't be a problem. I'll find you some clothes. You can take a shower if you like."

Despite Emily's nerves, she was flattered by his hospitality. She didn't expect it from such an angry seeming man. She took another sip of tea as the farmer stole another gaze at her. She felt heat rise in her cheeks. What was he thinking about? *What a state of a woman? I can't believe she fell over and then tried to chase cows in heels?* Emily looked down. The farmer left the room and came back two minutes later with a towel and a small pile of folded clothes.

"Sorry, they probably won't fit, but it'll be better than that." He indicated her ruined black pencil skirt and her torn silk white blouse. She put down her mug and gratefully accepted the pile of linen.

"Thank you." She smiled. He didn't return the gesture.

"It's this way." He led her through the kitchen and pointed upstairs. She had a moment of doubt. Feeling frozen she gazed at his face. You shouldn't judge a book by its cover but he didn't look like the murderous type. When Emily saw mug shots of killers on TV she was never surprised because they had a look about them, a look this one didn't have. He was a stranger but her car was broken anyway. If he wanted to hurt her it wasn't like she could get far whether she stayed here or not, she was in the middle of nowhere. She wasn't even sure if she could find her way back to Addleton, so she took her chances and climbed the stairs. He pointed to a room on the far side of the landing.

"Bathroom's in there, bedroom's in there," he indicated a door on the right. I'm going to make something to eat if you want to come down in a bit."

"Thank you." Emily smiled. As the man turned and went downstairs Emily breathed relief and walked into the bathroom. It was quite small, farmhouse style she supposed, but charming. It had a porcelain sink, free standing bath and stone walls. It wasn't like her bathroom back home but this wasn't the time to be picky. It was chilly and she bent to turn up the little radiator beside the bath. There was a curtain which could be drawn around the bath and a shower head above it. Emily drew the curtain and turned on the water. She placed the pile of linen on a little chair in the corner and faced the mirror. She really was a picture. Her hair was a state, most of it had come loose from her bun and was hanging bedraggled around her red and mud spattered face. She unpinned her bun and let her hair fall sweeping it to one side. Reaching into her handbag she pulled out a makeup wipe and began to clean away the smudged mascara and lipstick. She unbuttoned her blouse and cast it aside then unzipped her skirt and let it fall. Feeling suddenly embarrassed at the thought of being naked in a stranger's home she double checked the door was locked and then removed her underwear.

Emily climbed into the bath and let the stream of hot shower water run down over her body. She rinsed her hair and scrubbed at her ankles and feet. She found some shower gel by the side of the bath and worked it into her hair. How intimately embarrassing, using a stranger's shower gel. It smelled of apples. She didn't mind it. She rubbed it over her body and scrubbed away the mud flinching as she grazed her elbow. Emily twisted her arm to get a better look and was shocked to see a broad, red cut. It stung as she rinsed it. The water was dyed faintly red as it ran off her elbow. She'd have to ask the farmer for some antiseptic.

She finished up and towelled off then held up his shirt to her body. It was massive, its dark green plaid faded with use. Emily couldn't help herself; she sniffed it. It smelled fine, not sweaty like she was somehow expecting. It smelled clean with a tiny hint of men's aftershave. She put it on, carefully sliding it over her elbow and buttoning it up. Mark crossed her mind and she felt very aware she was wearing another man's shirt. She rolled the sleeves up until they were above her wrists. Emily comforted herself in the fact she was sure Mark would rather her wear the farmer's shirt than her torn blood stained blouse. She held up the jogging bottoms, and now she wondered how she could face the farmer wearing his huge baggy clothes and act normal about it when she still didn't even know his first name. She pulled on the grey bottoms and almost laughed when she saw how loose they were at her waist. She bent to roll up the ankles. Luckily she was tall at five foot nine. She tugged the draw strings as far as they would go and tied them in a knot. Emily had to admit she was pretty comfortable. She flicked her hair forward and wrapped it in the towel, bundling it on top of her head. She opened the bathroom door. The smell of food wafted up the stairs, and a sudden feeling of painful hunger gripped her. It was easy to forget that she was wearing the farmer's baggy clothes as she followed the smell downstairs.

At the bottom of the stairs, Emily found a large cosy lounge with a fire roaring in the grate. She turned right which led back to the sitting room and the adjacent open plan farmhouse kitchen. She looked across the room to see the farmer stirring a pot. It smelled heavenly. He was wearing a worn looking dark hoody and muddy jeans. He turned his head to look at her. She thought she caught a smirk on his lips before he turned back to the pot.

Crossing the room she passed another open fire and sat down at the kitchen table. She listened to the wooden spoon stirring in the pan. She heard the fire crackle and spark in the grate, felt its warmth close to her back. She had never been in a house like this before. It was charming; so much nicer than the town houses she was used to. Sure, she saw some big, prestigious ones, but this was so homely. Emily's apartment was minimalist and that was how she had thought she liked things until she set eyes on this farmhouse. It was easy to overlook the trail of mud on the kitchen floor and the dust which lingered on unpolished surfaces. The whole place was a little sad but still somehow comforting. Maybe it was the dimmed lights or the smell of home cooked food.

"Hungry?" the farmer mumbled, quietly disturbing Emily's daydream.

"Starving actually." Emily was almost sad the silence was broken and the magical calm was replaced by a tenser atmosphere. Maybe it was because the man still didn't sound happy. He took two bowls down from the cupboard and filled them with the wonderful smelling soup. He placed one down in front of her and one opposite.

"Would you like a drink?" he asked gruffly, avoiding eye contact.

"I'd love a glass of water, thank you," Emily replied, not wanting to be a bother by asking for anything that would require his effort.

He placed the glass down in front of her, along with a spoon.

"It smells amazing," she said, eager to break the silence. "I didn't get your name by the way."

He looked at her again with that brooding stare as if he were considering whether to give his name or not.

"It's Rome Buckley." He dipped his spoon into his soup taking a mouthful.

"My name's Emily Rogers."

"Nice to meet you," he said, quietly, keeping his gaze fixed on his food.

"I'm very sorry about the gate and your cows getting out like that and the confusion about not being who you thought I was." Emily tried an apology.

Rome Buckley looked up at her. "Don't worry about it. It's not a major problem."

"Then why do I get the feeling I've done something to make you angry?" she asked.

"It's not you. Really. It's complicated. We need a farm hand now. Seth has broken his leg and it's only me and him here, I can't manage it all by myself. We've never needed a farm hand before so I have no idea where to find one. I thought you were it, until of

course I saw you chase those cows in your stilettos."
Was that a smile tugging at his lips?

"I didn't expect to be chasing huge wild animals. I just came to view the farm for an hour, take some pictures and leave. I really didn't plan for this," Emily explained. Rome didn't reply, his only communication being a barely noticeable eyebrow raise. Emily wondered for a second who Seth was, thinking maybe he and Rome were brothers, but she wasn't sure how many more questions she could ask him before he became annoyed. He ate his soup, and Emily began to eat hers. It tasted as good as it smelled. Emily didn't know why she found herself surprised that the man could cook, but she was.

Rome

Rome watched Emily take delicate mouthfuls of the soup he'd made for her. He couldn't help but stare at her in his clothes. They draped off her slight frame. She was stunning, there was no doubt about it. Her blond hair was wrapped up in a towel, revealing her cheek bones, skin shining clean after her shower. She was delicate and sort of refined; how had he ever thought she was the farm hand? That bastard had sent her, it was obvious, but he couldn't think about him now otherwise he'd lose his cool and end up going over there. Instead he thought about his soup.

The woman kept trying to start a conversation with him. He appreciated that she must be feeling awkward and nervous but he had offered her a room, clothes, a shower and food, what more did she want? He finished his soup and opened a beer.

He needed more than beer. He wanted a bottle of whisky, but it didn't seem polite with the woman sitting opposite him. He looked past her at his dogs lying by the fire curled around each other, furry black and white ears twitching. Emily broke the silence again.

"Thank you, that was amazing." She pushed her bowl forward and sipped her water. He took the bowls to the sink and turned to her.

"Is there anything else you need?"

She shook her head and stood up from the table as if she were about to leave but then looked back at him.

"Actually, do you have any antiseptic cream?"

"Why? Are you okay?" Rome asked, his eyebrows knitting into a frown. He watched her roll up the sleeve of his green shirt and turn her arm so he could see her elbow. She had cut it, it looked quite bad. Feeling guilty, he moved over to her and gently touched her arm to examine it.

"Was that from chasing the cows?"

"No." She cleared her throat and looked at the floor. "When I fell over."

Rome nodded and walked over to the medicine cabinet. Every self-respecting farmer had a medicine cabinet. He dug through the cupboard until he found the antiseptic cream and a large plaster dressing. She smiled and thanked him again as he passed it to her. He watched her try to hold her arm at an angle and undo the lid of the antiseptic.

"Do you need a hand?"

Emily looked up at him with raised eyebrows but handed him back the cream and plaster. He undid the lid and peeled the plaster apart then covered the pad in the cream. He took her arm gently in one hand and placed the plaster over the cut, carefully smoothing down the edges to make sure it stuck properly. He could smell his shower gel in her hair. Sweet apples.

"There," he said. "I'll call the mechanic tomorrow. There's one down in the village. I don't know a lot about cars but I'm sure he'll get it fixed up."

"I'm really grateful, thank you. You've been really kind." She smiled sweetly at him. It was a reserved but warm smile. He still didn't return one.

"If you do need something you can knock on my door," Rome said. "It's the one up the stairs to the right. Sleep well." He whistled his dogs away from the fire, over to the other side of the kitchen where he poured them some food out. He waited for Emily to leave, watching her go and unable to hold back a smirk at his baggy jogging bottoms and shirt hanging from her.

Emily

Emily walked up the stairs and went to retrieve her bag from the bathroom. She took the towel off her head and rubbed her hair to almost dry, then brushed it out with the brush she had in her handbag. She rubbed some moisturiser into her face and hands, then left and opened the door to the room Rome had said she could sleep in. It was pretty, with a thick white bedspread with little blue flowers. The curtains matched. She closed the door and latched it behind her. Rome didn't seem dangerous, but she wasn't taking any chances.

There was a little bedside table and a chair by the bay window. A full length mirror stood opposite the bed. On the chair she noticed some more clothes: some jeans. Emily held them up and saw that they were women's jeans. They were even in her size. She assumed Rome had left them for her for the morning. Where had he gotten women's jeans from? She climbed into the bed and rested her head down. Now that everything was still and quiet she noticed the throbbing in her elbow more intensely. She'd held her breath as he'd put the plaster on. No one had ever done anything like that for her before. Even so, Emily still couldn't decide if he was a gentleman or just a stormy farmer. She reached down beside the bed and took out her phone. No signal, no way to contact Mark and it was already ten o'clock. She really didn't have the energy to go in search of an elusive phone signal. She was exhausted.

Emily awoke the next morning in a cloud of confusion as she opened her eyes and saw the unfamiliar bedroom. It took a few seconds for the memories of Rome Buckley and the cows to come to her. She yawned and stretched, then picked up her phone. Still no signal. Emily walked over to the curtains and drew them apart.

She was taken aback by the view. The morning sunshine bathed the lower valley in yellow light. The green hills sloped down to an area of shimmering water. It was in the distance but Emily could see the sun dazzling on the surface. Below her was a large garden attached to the farmhouse. Overgrown but large. Just beyond the thickly vegetated garden there was a small cottage nestled out of the way. Her estate agent mind began to work as she planned what she would do with this place to get it sold. She remembered Rome's reaction to that, though. It looked like her expertise wouldn't be needed here. She needed to get home and back to normality as soon as she could; imagine the commission she could be losing out on from those luxury London apartments.

Emily made her way out to the bathroom and sorted herself out. She threw her hair up into a messy bun, then pulled on the jeans Rome had left for her. They fitted perfectly. Looking down at Rome's oversized shirt she decided to tie a knot at the bottom so it wasn't so baggy. She put on some lip gloss and mascara, then highlighted her cheeks a little.

She headed downstairs. There was no sign of Rome. Maybe he was still asleep. She put the kettle on and made herself a cup of tea. The back door opened in that moment, causing her to jump a little. Rome walked in, covered in mud and hay. He wore a faded, plaid shirt with a hole in the arm and muddy jeans ripped at the thigh. He smelled like cows and something else a bit sickly sweet. She must have made an involuntary face.

"It's silage and cow crap," he explained.

"I…" she stuttered, trying to find some words. He actually smiled a little at her then but it faded quicker than it had arrived.

"I'd love a coffee," he said, as he walked his dogs over to the other side of the kitchen to feed them. They trotted past Emily as if she weren't there, following straight after their owner. Emily began making a coffee. It was the least she could do after he'd let her stay the night. Rome walked over to the sink to wash his hands. Emily watched as the water turned brown and thick dirt ran down the drain. She couldn't imagine her own hands being so muddy; it was as if he'd gone out on the farmyard and purposely bathed in the stuff.

"How's your elbow?" he asked.

She hadn't thought about it until now. "Fine, I think, thank you."

She watched him dry his hands on a tea towel.

"You should probably take that plaster off now. Let the air get to it," he suggested. He finished drying his hands and walked over to her. Being a head taller than she was she had to look up at him when they stood close together.

"May I?" Rome asked, reaching his hands out for the sleeve of her shirt. Emily nodded and then watched as he rolled up her sleeve. She felt his rough, calloused hands graze her forearm. They made her arm look stick-like in comparison. He gently peeled the plaster back and examined the cut, his dark curls falling over his forehead as he gazed down.

"It's not too bad," he said. "A bit bruised. You really fell hard." He hadn't even seen the bruise on her backside. Just then there was a knock at the door. It opened with a bang, accompanied by a woman's voice calling out.

"Rome, are you in?"

Emily was sure she saw his face tighten. He let her arm go brusquely, but not roughly, and took a noticeable step back from her.

"In here, Georgina," Rome said, but the woman had already made her way through to the kitchen. Her eyes found Emily instantly.

"And who might this be?" she asked in an unmistakably accusing tone with arms crossed in front of her. Her lips thinned into a straight line as she looked at Rome. She had a long brown ponytail and was wearing riding boots and jodhpurs Emily noticed as she looked her up and down scornfully.

"And in your shirt, no less." The woman's face grew harder. Emily felt her cheeks flame.

"It's not what it looks like Georgina. Really." Rome's face looked calm enough, but Emily could see how tense his body was.

"I'd love to hear your explanation before I just jump right to the wrong conclusion." The woman's piercing green eyes took in Emily's face, and Emily felt the heat intensify in her cheeks. She had no idea what to say as she watched the hostile scene play out. This was clearly Rome's girlfriend. Emily standing in Rome's kitchen early in the morning while wearing his shirt didn't exactly convey the best message.

"This is Emily Rogers. She's an estate agent. She came to value the farm," Rome assured the woman. "She helped me with some cows last night and got covered in mud. Hence the borrowing of the clothes. Her car also broke on her way down the track. Hence the car in the track."

The woman raised her eyebrows but her expression remained cold.

"Maybe we can talk in private?" she said, flicking a glance over at Emily.

Emily realised that she wasn't wanted. "Of course, sorry."

Emily rushed off round the corner to the bottom of the stairs but being unable to help herself she lingered there. Her mother had always told her she was far too nosy for her own good. She peeked through the crack in the door by the hinges. The woman was clearly furious, while Rome seemed just as grumpy as usual from what Emily had seen of him so far.

"I don't know why you acted so shocked to see this woman when it was clearly you who sent her." Rome looked at Georgina, who still had her arms crossed. She scowled at Rome's comment.

"I had nothing to do with it. If she really is an estate agent as you say, then it's probably just Daddy giving you a kick up the arse."

"There are politer ways to do so than sending an estate agent all the way from London without giving me an ounce of warning," said Rome, glowering down at Georgina.

"You know Daddy," said Georgina, tossing her ponytail and looking up at Rome.

"This really beats all of his previous attempts at rattling me and Seth. I mean, he's sparing no expense to go all out to make our lives difficult. The estate agent came all the way from London for God's sake. He couldn't have chosen one closer to annoy me?" Rome shook his head; the anger hadn't left his voice as he vented his frustrations.

Georgina shrugged. "You know that Daddy only deals with the best, and they're a good firm. It's irrelevant anyway; I'm sure you told the woman she wasn't needed. It's not like the farm's going on the market right now."

Rome stood silently for a while as he scuffed his work boot on the wooden floor.

"Anyway I didn't come here for an argument. I came to see if you'll come out for dinner tonight at *The Stag*," Georgina asked.

"I'm very busy right now with the farm, Georgina," Rome said. "You know lambing season is starting and I don't have any help. Seth is out of action and he's the one that knows most about it. Normally he takes the lead."

"Oh Rome, you can come once you've finished the animals. Just dinner. I hardly get to see you." Georgina reached out her hands and placed them on each of his arms.

"I'll see what I can do," Rome said. "I have to get going now, though. Lots to do." He leant forward and kissed Georgina briefly on the lips, then led her to the door with a hand on her lower back.

Emily couldn't believe she had just spied on them. She knew she was much too curious, some might say nosy. She didn't mean any harm, though. She tiptoed up the stairs, and then ran back down loud enough to be heard, just to be sure Rome didn't suspect her of eavesdropping.

"Sorry about that, it seems I'm bringing you endless drama," Emily said. Rome was by the kettle, making his own coffee. Emily took in the smells of the farm kitchen: the silage and cow smell, Rome's dogs. She guessed that people grew to overlook it after years on a farm. The smell of Rome's coffee masked it a little.

"She'll get over it," said Rome, bluntly, as he took a gulp of coffee. He changed the subject; he clearly didn't want to discuss the woman. "I've called Darren, the mechanic, and he's towing your car to the garage this morning so we'll see what the damage is."

"Thank you, I'm really grateful for your help."

"Now, I've got a lot to get on with," Rome said. "You can stay here or come out and give me a hand."

Emily froze for a second. The last thing she wanted to do was come face to face with more animals, but it seemed rude to decline his offer. "Right, sure. I'll come out."

Emily had no experience of the countryside having always lived in towns and cities. Her parents were divorced so she had been cast around a lot. Emily's father worked as a lawyer so they'd always had enough money. A few years after the divorce her father had moved out to America and Emily was forced to live with her crazy mother who worked as a marriage councillor. A lot of good that had done her when it came to her divorcing Emily's father.

Emily was adaptable though; that was one personality trait she had always liked about herself. She could get thrown into anything and she'd give it a good go. That was why she was out here, wasn't it? She'd driven from her apartment in London to come and value this farm because her boss had decided she'd be able to manage it. She was giving it her best shot no matter how strangely things had turned out. Thank God it was a Saturday, otherwise she'd be explaining to her boss that she couldn't go back to work because her car had ground out on the farm track and then she'd have to tell him how she hadn't even done her job yet but instead was chasing cows around the place with a hunky, moody farmer. She tried not to laugh at the thought of her boss's reaction.

Rome walked through the kitchen door, out into the entry hall and went into a cupboard. He reappeared blowing some dust off a pair of wellies.

"Here, these might do." He handed her the boots. She snatched her hands back away from the offer and peeked inside them. She looked gingerly up at Rome.

"Will you check them for spiders?" Rome raised an eyebrow, then tipped them upside down and banged them together. To Emily's satisfaction, nothing fell out.

"Thanks." Emily slipped them on. They did fit; this man was strangely good at guessing clothing sizes. They went out the front door into the outhouse where Rome pulled a coat down from a hook. He handed it to her.

"Still pretty cold in the mornings," he said.

Emily slipped it on. It was checked and red, she felt like a lumber jack, but it was comfy and warm too. She didn't think she'd ever worn such comfy clothes. It was all heels and pencil skirts in the office.

They made their way out on to the farmyard. Emily could take it all in now in the daylight. Cattle barns stood to the left of them. Rolling hills, misted with dew, sloped upwards ahead of them. The tree-lined lane led towards her broken car. Daffodils pierced the ground along the verge lines as they began to grow up to meet the sun. It wasn't what Emily was used to, but she could appreciate the beauty.

The morning was crisp and bright and the sun was rising as they turned left and walked down past the cattle barns towards a fence line. Another big shed was ahead and beyond was the lower valley falling away towards the stretch of water that Emily had seen from her window.

She took out her phone to see if she had any signal out here. Still none.

"You won't get much signal on that thing out here," confirmed Rome, apparently reading her mind.

"Is there *anywhere* with signal around here?" Emily asked hopefully.

"Yeah, the village. Oh, and one spot at the top of the valley. Occasionally I manage to get some in the kitchen." Rome gave a short laugh.

"How will I call my boss?"

"You could walk up the valley later if it's that important. Or just wander around the farm for a bit until you find a bar," Rome suggested. He wasn't looking at her but ahead at the barn they were approaching.

"Right, okay," she said, as she tried to match his pace across the yard. Emily put her phone back in her pocket. She would have to find a signal later; all she wanted to do was get hold of her boss before she made a bad name for herself in the office and missed out on the important promotion.

"What are we doing then?" she asked.

"We're sorting the lambing shed," he replied.

"What's lambing?" Emily asked a little out of breath. Rome stopped abruptly in the yard and turned to face her, almost causing Emily to crash straight into him.

"What's lambing?" He actually seemed amused. Emily scuffed her boot on the floor as she stared down at the ground.

"Do I look like the kind of girl who knows what lambing is?"

He smiled. "You look like the kind of gal who's about to learn what it is. Come on." He continued walking towards the barn. "We have to empty out all this farming equipment and then set up hurdle pens ready for the ewes."

"Ewes?" Emily asked. Rome's eyebrows raised higher than she'd seen them go so far.

"You don't know what a ewe is?" Rome seemed genuinely surprised now. Emily stared at him. Why this man expected her to know all of these strange farming terms she didn't know. "A ewe is a sheep. Lambing is when the ewes come in to the barn and give birth to baby sheep. A cow is a big black and white thing with horns."

"I know what a cow is thank you," said Emily, with a sarcastic smile. "So they can't just have their babies in the field?"

"Some farmers do it that way," Rome explained, "but Seth and I like to keep a close eye on them and it can be tough on the lambs down in the valley where it's wet. We like to give them a head start where they can grow stronger."

Emily nodded then whipped her head round at the sound of a crash at the back of the shed.

"Bugger it!" A man's voice said.

"Seth?" Rome called.

"Yeah it's me," the voice called back.

"What are you doing out here? You're meant to be resting," Rome called.

A man appeared from behind a tractor. He was tall, but not quite as tall as Rome. He had dark hair and stubble. He was handsome but in more of a sweet way, not as rugged and broad as Rome, at least in Emily's opinion. He was on crutches and had one leg in a cast.

"I was just trying to get some hurdles out. We need to sort the barn," Seth said.

"I can manage, Seth. Get back indoors and rest," said Rome.

"And who's this?" Seth gestured to Emily, ignoring Rome's concern.

"Her name's Emily and she's *not* the new farm hand," Rome said, glancing back at her and smiling. "Long story. Anyway, we're about to sort this mess out. I'll give you a shout later when it's time to get the sheep in. You can stand somewhere while I round them up."

"*Someone's* happy to give orders now I'm out of action." Seth raised his eyebrows. Rome laughed.

"You'll just have to get used to it won't you," Rome smiled.

"Only for six weeks. It's only been a few days and I've had enough already."

Emily noticed his sunken eyes and thought he looked a little tired.

"It'll fly by." Rome patted Seth on the shoulder. "I've got this, you can trust me."

"You know I trust you, I just hate not being able to work."

"I know. Get back inside and rest though. I'll come and find you later," said Rome.

"All right, nice to meet you, Emily." Emily and Seth exchanged smiles before he reluctantly hobbled away on his crutches.

"He hates not being able to work and boss me around," laughed Rome.

*

Emily had been watching Rome use a tractor to drive some trailers out of the barn. He had used the thing on the front to pick up some bales and move them out. They had been out there for about half an hour and Emily hadn't really done much yet.

"You want a go?" Rome called from the cab window. Emily laughed. She shook her head.

"Come on, it's fun."

"I'm not driving that. I don't like driving as it is; I'm not getting in a tractor," she called over the noise of the engine.

"I'll teach you," Rome insisted, staring at her.

Emily looked at the huge tractor; the back wheels were taller than her. The thought of being in control of that much metal was daunting.

"When will you ever get the chance again? Honestly, after seeing you chase the cows I thought you'd be up for this," Rome called.

She couldn't believe she was even considering it. He was right, though, when would she ever get another chance? Maybe it was about time she finally faced her fear. One of her fears, anyway. What better way to do it than getting in one of the biggest vehicles Emily had ever seen?

She reluctantly stepped into the barn and approached the tractor. Rome jumped down from the cab and stepped aside, raising a hand to direct her up the steps. Emily looked at him for a second before climbing up and sitting in the driver's seat. It bounced up and down and she made a little 'o' shape with her mouth and grabbed the steering wheel.

"They've got good suspension," Rome said, with a laugh. Emily watched him climb in after her and perch on the little passenger seat.

"Right. Those are the gears. That's the clutch, the accelerator, the brake. I hope you know where the steering wheel is." He pointed to each one in turn. "Now, you just flick this back and forwards to go into reverse, neutral and forwards. You hold the clutch down as you do it, think of it just the same as your car. The gear stick has buttons; you just click up or down to go faster or slower. It's pretty bouncy so you don't really want to brake too hard or anything and you can just drive it round the back and park it outside the cattle shed. Got it?" It was probably more words than he'd said in total to her since she'd been here.

"I think so," Emily said, blowing out a breath. She grabbed the steering wheel and looked out of the huge windscreen. The ground was far away. Emily didn't know if it was scary to be so high or more of a comfort knowing she would be safer in this huge tractor than in a little car. She put her foot down on the clutch and flipped the orange lever forwards out of neutral.

Emily took a deep breath and lifted her foot off the clutch. The tractor lurched forwards, sending them both out their seats. She bounced back down into the springy chair and set her foot back down on the clutch gasping as she looked at Rome. He was smiling, but Emily didn't find it funny in the slightest.

"Don't worry about it," he said. "Go again."

What was she doing? Emily took a deep breath and lifted her foot off again, slower this time. The tractor still lunged forward but it was a little more controlled. Her foot was completely off the clutch now and they were moving forwards. She couldn't help but look at Rome and smile even though they were going slower than walking pace. He reached across her and clicked the gears up. His arm brushed hers as he drew it back. The tractor sped up and Emily steered them towards the cattle shed.

They bounced over potholes and made their way steadily across the yard. Emily managed to brake to a halt outside the barn causing them both to jolt forwards in their seats as the tractor bounced to a stop. Rome flicked the orange lever into neutral. He cranked up the hand brake on the floor between them as Emily let out a shaky breath and rubbed her sweaty palms on her jeans. It wasn't as bad as she thought it was going to be.

"Grand job," Rome announced as he opened the door to jump out. Emily got out of the cab and climbed down the precariously steep steps to follow him. She looked over at Rome and they smiled at each other.

"I can't believe I just did that," she breathed.

"Wasn't so nerve wracking, was it?" he asked.

"I don't know, I was pretty scared," Emily admitted.

"I get the feeling you really don't like driving," said Rome. "You said you were going to stay in a hotel last night instead of driving back in the dark."

"Honestly, it petrifies me," said Emily, as they both turned and walked towards the lambing shed.

"What do you find so scary about it?" Rome asked.

Emily's heart beat a little faster and she felt her palms sweat. She didn't like talking about her fear of driving. She didn't like to think about it.

"You okay?" asked Rome. Emily realised she had ignored his question.

"Oh, yes. It's … well … something happened a long time ago that put me off," Emily cleared her throat. She could say it, it wasn't a big deal. "I was in a car crash, quite a bad one. I spent some time in hospital, broke some bones. In fact, they weren't sure if they were going to be able to save me."

She felt her stomach turn as she said the words. When the nurse had told Emily she was lucky to be alive it had made her realise that she never wanted to drive again. Slowly, she had built up the confidence to get back in a car but the fear had always been there.

As Emily told Rome about the car crash she watched his expression fade into a dark one. He was silent for a few seconds, before he cleared his throat and raked a hand through his dark curls as they continued across the yard.

"I'm very sorry you went through that. If I'd known I never would have pressured you to get in the tractor," he said, with a sympathetic smile.

"No don't be silly. I think it was easier than being in a car actually. It feels safe in there. Like you're driving a tank." Emily laughed, trying to lighten the mood.

"Aye, there is that," said Rome.

They spent the next hour dragging hurdles out from the back of the barn and setting up little square pens for the newborn lambs. Rome said the newborns were best kept separate from the rest of the flock for a few days so they didn't get trampled. The work was hard but Emily felt good spending the day outdoors doing something useful. Farm work wasn't as bad as she had expected it to be, although she was very aware of the fact that her manicure had been chipped to pieces.

They put buckets in the hurdle pens, ready to fill with water. They left one big area for the sheep to come into once they got them in from the field. Rome explained the sheep would have their lambs over a few weeks but not all at the same time, so they didn't all need a separate pen.

"Shall we head in and get some lunch?" he suggested and smoothed his hand over his forehead, wiping away sweat. They had both discarded their coats a while back, leaving them hanging from a gate.

"Sounds good," Emily said, and followed him in.

Rome

Rome walked through to the kitchen and put the kettle on. He stretched his arms up, trying to relieve the ache in his biceps. They had worked hard out there; now all he could think about was demolishing the food he was about to make and then going out to get the sheep in. He got a loaf of bread from the bread bin and a pack of sausages from the fridge.

"Not a vegetarian or anything, are you?" he called to Emily, praying she would say no. He had no idea what to feed one of them.

"No," she called back. He could hear her in the entrance hall struggling with her boots. He was impressed at how hard she had worked today. He'd never seen that from a town girl before. She came through to the kitchen and he looked over to see her messy hair and baggy shirt. The jeans fitted her perfectly, just as he had thought they would. He'd known she was the same size as *her*. He washed and dried his hands.

"Take a seat, I can make us some sausage sandwiches." He grabbed a pan from the cupboard and chucked the sausages in with some oil.

"You have a very busy life," he heard her say from the kitchen table.

"Aye, I do," he agreed. She didn't know the half of it. He cut four slices of bread and arranged them on two plates. He slathered them in butter and ketchup. He hoped it wouldn't be too slapdash for her. He felt her watching him as he moved around the kitchen. He grabbed two mugs to make them tea and coffee. His dogs were sitting together behind him waiting for him to drop something.

"Go lie down, dogs," he said to them. They trotted off to the mat in front of the unlit fire. There was silence as Rome made their sandwiches. Maybe he'd been treating her a little too rudely but it wasn't like it mattered now. She'd be gone as soon as her car was fixed.

He brought two plates over to the table and then set their mugs down.

"Thank you." Emily smiled at him.

He took a bite out of his sandwich and watched as she delicately ate hers. He couldn't help but stare. She was beautiful. Her skin had a warm glow to it, while her light hair was soft and wavy as tendrils fell from her bun. She reminded him of *her,* but he didn't want to think about that now.

"That was fun; I can't believe I drove a tractor," she said, around a bite of her sandwich, pulling Rome out of his thoughts. Her blue eyes twinkled.

"You did a grand job, better than any townie I've ever seen," he said.

Emily laughed; it was sweet and feminine, certainly more feminine than the way she had fallen on his patio yesterday. The memory made him smile involuntarily. He sipped his coffee to hide his happiness with his mug. There was more than one reason why he didn't want to make friends with her.

They both finished off their sandwiches quickly, hungry from the work they had been doing all morning.

"I guess we'd better get back out there and get those bastard sheep in," Rome said.

"Sounds like you're not so keen."

"You'll soon see what a ball-ache it is once we get out there."

*

Ten minutes later they were making their way down to the valley with Tess and Birdie at their heels and Seth clicking along behind them with his crutches. Emily seemed to spend most of the time taking in the wide expanse of short green grass. She had probably never seen such big, open spaces before.

"Where do you want me?" Seth asked from behind them.

"You can stand by the gate and then when you see us coming just head back up the yard a bit and direct them down into the barn," Rome answered. "Emily and I will go down the valley with the dogs and round them up." He opened the wooden gate to the sloping pastures beyond.

Emily and Rome walked down the field together as the sun descended in the sky. They reached the stream and Rome chose a shallow part to cross. He watched as Emily picked her way over the rocks. The dogs splashed through the water and ran ahead wagging their tails. They reached the flock and Rome whistled his dogs into action. They circled round the back of the flock.

"Birdie, come-by," he called. "Tess, away." He watched them work quickly and obediently to gather the flock. He directed Emily over a few paces as the dogs ran the flock through the water and up the side of the valley. Water splashed as hundreds of sheep charged through. Nothing gave Rome greater pleasure than watching his dogs work. They loved it as much as he did.

"Birdie, come-by," he called. One of the sheep made a break from the flock and others started to follow. "Tess, away!" His trusted companion got the animal back in line. Rome was just thinking how unusually smoothly it was going when he heard a splash behind him. He whirled round to see Emily wallowing around in the stream. She coughed and looked over at him as she tried to get to her feet.

"Having a nice swim are we?" He couldn't help but laugh. "If you wanted a bath you could've had one back at the house."

Her eyebrows furrowed as she struggled to get to her feet. He walked over to help her up.

"Stand!" he called to his dogs who both lay down on the grass eagerly awaiting their next command. Emily had pulled herself off the ground and was on her hands and knees in the shallow water.

"Are you hurt?" He reached down and offered his hands, pulling her up.

She cleared her throat and took her hands back to sweep wet hair from her face.

"You fall over a lot, don't you?" said Rome.

"I can't believe I did it again," she said, covering her reddening face with her hands. She was dripping wet all down her front and she wrapped her arms tightly around herself.

"Come on, let's get you back." Rome slipped a hand round her back and guided her up the hill a little. The flock were beginning to separate and the dogs' ears were pricked ready to listen to their next order.

"Birdie come-by," he called. "Away. Away." The dogs worked the sheep up towards the gate at the top of the field. Rome moved across to block the sheep running up the valley as the dogs guided them closer.

"Will you just stand over to your right?" he called to Emily. He watched her jog over.

"Just wave your arms at them like you did with the cows. You're doing a grand job." He was impressed at how she took his orders on board and got the job done, even if she couldn't stay on her own two feet. The flock got through the gate and Seth waved a crutch to direct them down into the lambing shed.

"That'll do," Rome called to the dogs. He took up the rear and swung the gate round on the sheep. He ruffled the fur on Tess and Birdie's heads. "Good girls, good girls."

"Lovely job," he said, turning to look at Emily. "Why don't you take yourself indoors while I sort these out? There's some more clothes in the airing cupboard at the top of the stairs."

He watched as she trudged off to the house and then he turned to Seth.

"I'm telling you, that gal's got some drive for a city lass," he said, smiling.

"So, who is she then?" asked Seth, leaning on his crutches. Rome dangled his forearms over the sheep gate and sighed. He felt anger building in him once again.

"That bastard sent her to value the farm," Rome said, darkly.

"No, really?" Seth said. "Has she done it?"

"No, she didn't get a chance after her car broke on her," Rome said, turning to face Seth.

"He's taken it to another level this time. How far is he going to go? What will we do?" Seth raked a hand through his hair, his face creasing with worry but by the steely line of his jaw Rome could tell he was as angry as he was.

"The winning question. I was going to ask you the same thing." Rome looked down and scuffed his boot on the sparse, black gravel.

"Any luck finding a farm hand yet?" Seth was clearly trying to steer the conversation away from their biggest problem towards a smaller one. Seth lifted an arm, crutch attached, and scratched his head. Rome shook his head. He'd not managed to bring himself to call Mandy back yet to see if there was anyone else she could send after the first one had failed to turn up.

"I suppose we'd struggle to find anyone willing to do it for what we can afford to pay them anyway," Rome said.

"They'd be getting a place to live and they'd be fed. What more could they want?"

The men chuckled. Rome knew exactly how few people an offer like that would attract.

"I've got to head out anyway. Georgina wants me to go out to *The Stag* with her. Keep an ear out for the sheep won't you?" said Rome.

"Sure," Seth cleared his throat and then looked Rome in the eyes. "How long is Emily staying?"

"Just until her car's back on the road. It's a long cab journey back otherwise. She was actually a big help today," Rome admitted.

"Maybe we should keep her on as a farm hand then," joked Seth.

"It's better than any ideas I've had so far."

"I don't know how Georgina would feel about that, mind."

Rome raised his eyebrows in response.

"Let's try not to worry too much. Anyway, we'll think of something, we always do. Have fun with

Georgina. I'll see you tomorrow." Seth hobbled off towards the cottage. Rome walked through to the farmhouse. He washed his hands and then headed upstairs for a shower. He burst through the bathroom door without thinking and jumped at the sound of a shriek.

"Oh my God!" the voice yelled.

"God, sorry!" He slammed the door shut quickly and stood there for a moment, eyes scrunched shut.

"I didn't see anything," he called through the closed door. He heard the shower turn off and the bath thud as Emily clambered out. He raked his hand anxiously through his hair.

"The curtain is see-through," she squeaked. Well he knew that, it was *his* shower.

"I didn't look, I wasn't paying attention," he assured her. He'd completely forgotten he was sharing his house. The door opened and Emily emerged, wrapped in a white towel, hair dripping down her back, red-faced. She flicked her eyes to meet his and quickly away again as she rushed past. Sweet apples filled his nostrils and he turned to watch her rush to her door. The towel dipped under her shoulder blades revealing the smooth wet skin down to her lower back. He averted his gaze quickly.

"Sorry," he called after her, but she had already disappeared into her bedroom and slammed the door behind her.

Rome opened the bathroom door and was shrouded in warm shower steam. He pulled his shirt off over his head and undid his belt buckle, whipping it off and undressing. He took his razor out of the cupboard and shaved his face close to the skin to remove a few days' worth of stubble. Rome smoothed his jawline with his fingers and looked into the mirror. He sighed; he looked tired. It wasn't surprising; he had a lot on his mind. There was too much to sort out and not enough time. Too much in his head.

He climbed into the bath tub and turned on the shower taking a breath as the water slid down his tired, aching body. He rubbed shower gel into his skin, over his biceps and chest. He worked his way down his body. The nostalgic scent filled his mind and after the last few months of trying desperately to hold it in and keep himself together he felt a sudden prick of emotion in his chest. He let a tear fall down his cheek. It was swept away by the water, for no one to see but him. He closed his eyes and inhaled as the familiar feeling of sadness gripped him. He took some deep breaths; he just didn't have time to let himself feel these things right now.

"Get a hold of yourself," he whispered, as he rubbed his hands firmly down his face, banishing the weakness.

Emily

Emily dried her hair furiously with the bath towel. Never had she embarrassed herself more in front of a man, in front of anyone. First, she had fallen over in front of his house. Then, she had made a fool of herself chasing cattle. After that, she had almost sent them through the windscreen of a tractor and of course "went for a swim", in his stream. Now, to top it all off, he'd seen her naked.

She felt like leaving before he got out of the bathroom. She could just walk until she found civilization and a phone signal then call a cab to take her back to her apartment. There, she could pretend her trip here had never happened. She could try and explain to her boss about the mishap with her car and how Mr Buckley didn't want his farm valued after all. She could go back to work on Monday as if this had never happened, as if she hadn't met the most attractive but confusing man she'd ever laid eyes on. He was laughing one minute, grumpy with her the next.

She should absolutely not be attracted to him. Firstly, he was with Georgina, and Emily wasn't the kind of woman who even thought about men who were spoken for. Secondly, she had Mark to go back to. Mark. Why didn't she miss him? Why did it scare her to admit that?

Emily brushed her hair out and put Rome's jogging bottoms back on, along with another shirt she had found in the airing cupboard. She paced the room, trying to think of what she should do. She needed to find out when her car would be ready. She shouldn't stay another night. What would Mark be thinking? She was due back today, and she didn't want to stay here any longer. She wanted to get back to London, make up for lost time at work and ensure she was still in line for the promotion.

Emily had been going to drive the rest of the way back to London today, Saturday, after staying in a hotel for a night to save her driving back in the dark. She hadn't even made it to the hotel. She hadn't been able to call Mark. She'd sent a text but it hadn't got through; she still didn't have any signal. After having tried all around the house with no luck she had planned to walk up the valley as Rome had suggested but she'd got caught up doing the lambing shed and getting the sheep in. Emily looked out the window to see the sun was setting in the sky. She breathed a deep sigh as she thought about her list of problems.

A soft knock at her door disturbed her thoughts.

"Are you decent?" an Irish accent asked. She hoped that wasn't humour in his tone.

"Yes."

"So, can I come in then?" he asked.

"I suppose."

He opened the door and came into the room. Emily felt heat rise in her cheeks, caused by a rising feeling of embarrassment. She was taken aback by the sight. He'd shaved, and it accentuated his high cheek bones and dimpled chin. He was wearing dark jeans and a white, button-down Oxford shirt. His hair was damp and brushed to the side. Thick dark curls. Emily cleared her throat.

"Can I help you?" she prompted.

He raised his eyebrows as he said, "I just wanted to say sorry I burst in on you. I really didn't see anything."

Emily crossed her arms over her chest self-consciously.

He continued, "Your car still isn't done so you're welcome to stay the night again. There's a utility room downstairs if you need to wash any clothes. I'll probably be back a little late. Seth's in the cottage if you need anyone."

"Thank you. I'm going to have to get back tomorrow. I should have been back already. I have a busy life in London and I have work on Monday. If my car's not done then I'll have to find another way," Emily said.

"Sure. I can drive you back if your car's not done by then. I'll call the mechanic in the morning to check on the progress."

"It's a long way back to London, and you're very busy here," said Emily.

"I also feel to blame for you coming out here for no reason. I suppose you've wasted a lot of time and money," Rome said.

Emily smiled and nodded. They stood in silence for a second. "It's fine really; you've been kind enough to have me here when I don't have anywhere else to go. I was looking forward to the commission, though."

He smiled. "Feel free to stay tonight and we'll try and sort some things out tomorrow. I'd best get on before I get a battering from the woman." He smiled briefly and retreated out the door closing it behind him. "Help yourself to food," he called through the closed door.

Emily listened to Rome's Landrover crunch on the gravel outside as he drove off down the track and away from the farm. She gazed around the bedroom wondering what she should do now. She felt so awkward being here. She'd never planned on staying at a stranger's house. Then again, just as Rome had said, it wasn't her fault he didn't want his farm to be valued. It wasn't her fault he had a dodgy farm track which had broken her car and which she was now going to have to pay for.

She grabbed her phone and stuffed it into her pocket, then gathered up the little pile of dirty laundry she'd formed. It included her underwear from the first night, Rome's shirt and the jeans. She carried the pile downstairs to find the utility room. Emily decided that she would put those in the wash so she could at least wear underwear tomorrow, then she'd walk up the valley to find signal while there was still a fraction of daylight left.

*

An hour or so had passed since Rome had left for the pub, and Emily was somewhere near the top of the valley. It was dark now and getting a little colder. She pulled her coat tight around her and warily eyed her surroundings before calling Mark.

She was almost surprised when he picked up the phone. He was normally too busy.

"Emily?" his familiar voice said, on the other end of the line.

"Hi Mark. I was just calling to let you know where I was. I ended up having to stay at the farm I was valuing because my car broke. I couldn't make it to the hotel."

"So, when will you be back?" he asked sounding a little far away.

"Hopefully tomorrow so I can make it to work on Monday. If my car isn't fixed in time the farmer has offered to give me a lift."

"Are you sure you should be staying with a stranger?" Emily could tell by his tone he was distracted as usual.

"I'll be fine," she said, shortly, as she scraped at a tuft of grass with the toe of her welly.

"All right, that's good then." There was a pause and Emily heard some shuffling around. "Okay Emily, I'll see you when you get back."

The line went dead. Emily checked the bars in the corner of her phone screen to see she had good signal. He had hung up then.

Emily wasn't surprised that he sounded like he didn't miss her. Things weren't at their best right now. But she didn't want her life to change yet, not after four years of being with him. They would just have to push through their difficulties. Flicking her phone torch on she began to carefully navigate her way down the rutted hillside.

Emily shone her phone torch so she could watch her footing as she reached the bottom of the hill and walked into the farmyard. She passed the cattle barns and heard the creatures shuffling around, chewing and snorting. As she reached the garden path she heard another noise, a bleating coming from ahead, down towards the lambing shed. Emily stood still and listened. It had stopped. As she opened the gate it began again. Did farmers check their animals whenever they heard a noise? She guessed there was no harm in going down to cast her eye over the flock. She wouldn't get in there and touch any; she'd just have a quick look.

Fastening a few more buttons on Rome's red coat, she made her way down to the lambing barn. Emily reached the gates and shone her torch over the flock. She didn't exactly know what she was looking for. The torch didn't reach far but she did her best to scan. There was a grunting noise and a baa. Angling her torch towards the noise she craned her neck forwards to scan the shed. It was too dark to see far enough. Emily didn't know anything about animals but she could tell there was a sheep in there that must be in some sort of distress. Oh God, she would have to go in.

With a tremble in her fingers she untied the gate and then retied it behind her as Rome had instructed after she had let the cows escape on the first night. She kept her back against the gate, flicking her torch around, making sure none of the animals were near her. She moved around the side of one sheep so she could get a more central view of her surroundings. The baa sounded again and she shone her torch over to see which one was making the sound. Finally Emily spied the culprit over at the back. If she wanted a better look she was going to have to move through the flock. She could do this. She had helped round them up in the field when they were all jumpy. They were just standing still now and they certainly weren't as scary as the cows.

Steadily, Emily shuffled on and the sheep parted until she reached the one which was bleating and grunting. It was laid on its side, away from the others. She could see its tummy was moving up and down hard as it breathed. Emily moved closer. It lifted its head to see her and wiggled its legs in an effort to stand but it didn't manage to. It definitely looked sick. Emily had no idea what she could do for the animal or even what was wrong with it. She didn't have Rome's number to call him to ask for help and even if she had it, she would have to find signal first. If the sheep was in danger then Emily needed to find help. Even she could tell there was something very wrong with it.

Seth sprang to mind. Rome had said if she needed anything she should knock on the cottage door. Emily had seen the cottage from her bedroom window. It was just beyond the farmhouse garden, not far from the lambing shed.

"I'll be right back," Emily promised the sheep, then left the barn, tying the gate behind her. She jogged left past the sheep barn, behind the overgrown farmhouse garden, to the little cottage. She knocked hard on the door and waited, tapping her fingers against her leg until it opened two minutes later. Seth stood before her on crutches. He looked tired. He had an old scruffy hoody on, along with baggy joggers so he could fit his cast in. He looked a little confused to see her.

"Sorry, did I wake you?" Emily lowered her phone torch, realising she was shining it in his face as he squinted.

"No, no it's fine. What wrong? Has something happened to Rome?" Seth's eyes seemed frozen open and fully alert as he stared into Emily's.

"No, actually, it's a sheep. It's probably fine but I heard lots of baas, you know? So I went to check it out and one of the sheep is on its side and it won't get up. It's making grunting noises. It's probably nothing, I've probably wasted your time." Emily was beginning to feel silly but Seth was already reaching for his coat. He pulled it on while standing on one leg, wobbling a little.

"You might be about to see your first lamb." Seth's eyes were bright as he grabbed hold of his crutches and nodded his head in the direction of the lambing barn, silently suggesting they make a move. They hurried to the shed. Emily untied the gate so Seth could hobble through.

"Thanks," he murmured, quietly, as he went through and started to move to the back of the shed. Emily followed with her torch. Seth approached the wall and flicked a switch. The strip lighting illuminated the shed. Emily had missed that before. Seth looked down at the sheep and Emily felt the anticipation rise as he checked the animal over.

"Yep," he confirmed. "It's in labour." Seth grinned at her but soon after his face fell. "Trust Rome to go out tonight of all nights," Seth complained. "How the hell am I going to pull this thing out on one leg? He scratched his head.

"So you have to pull the baby out?" Emily asked. She wished there was something she could do but she really knew nothing about it.

"If it gets stuck, yes. Otherwise the ewe and the lamb could die. This Dorset is a first timer. It's her first lamb so there's always the possibility for more complications."

Seth looked serious, his lips set in a thin line.

"What's a Dorset?" Emily asked.

"It's just the name for her breed. They have white faces and curly horns."

"What should we do?" Emily felt helpless as she gazed down at the sheep.

"It *might* go well. She might push it out on her own. She could be a while yet before she even wants to push it out," Seth confirmed, looking down at the panting animal.

"And what if it doesn't go well?" Emily felt panic unfurl in her stomach.

"Then I'll be watching you lamb your first ewe." Seth raised his eyebrows and smiled.

Emily's mouth opened and closed as she tried to formulate an answer.

"I've never even touched a sheep!" she said, wide-eyed, as her heart hammered in her chest.

"You'll be fine. I'll tell you what to do. You've given everything else a good go. Why not this?"

"Lives weren't at risk the last few times," Emily said, eyeing the sheep and feeling suddenly aware of the little animals wandering all around her.

"Lives are always at risk on a farm," Seth said. "We just have to try and do it as safely as possible." Seth wobbled round to the back end of the sheep. He stared down at the animal and then looked up at her. "You see there? That's the water bag. It looks like it won't be long now after all."

Emily's palms were sweating, blood rushed in her ears. She wasn't ready to do this. She never expected any of this to happen when she came to value this farm. She'd planned to sleep in her hotel room and drive back to her apartment in her perfect BMW.

Now she was going to pull a baby out of a sheep. She looked at Seth, wishing for a way out of this.

"What's a water bag?"

Emily listened closely as Seth explained what he called "the basics of lambing". It was not *basic*. He explained when they should intervene and when to pull, how to pull, where to put her hands. He told her what to do when it came out, what to do if it was stuck, what to do if it came out not breathing. He went over how to make it breathe and how to get it to drink.

Emily swallowed the lump in her dry throat. She felt a serious amount of pressure as she watched the sheep in the dim light of the barn. At first the other sheep had kept their distance but now a few nosy ones were beginning to take an interest and Emily kept feeling them nose at her back. She desperately tried to ignore their presence as she kept still and quiet in the straw like Seth had told her. He said if the sheep felt threatened or scared it might try to hold back its lamb and not push, which would put them in danger.

Seth was waiting patiently, leaning up against the stone barn wall. He watched the sheep intently before gazing over at Emily.

"So what do you think of life on the farm?" he murmured quietly.

"It's intense. Stressful," Emily admitted, nodding. But she also thought about the rolling valleys and the fresh farm air, once you got over the mix of strange farm smells. She thought about her stressful job back home and she could see the appeal of living out here in the country. She missed her phone, though, along with having shops nearby and clean underwear to put on.

"It's nice. It's pretty out here. Not so busy and loud." She twiddled a piece of straw round in her fingers. Seth nodded.

"Yep, it's definitely quiet," he agreed. Emily looked up at him. She thought this might be a chance to help her figure something out.

"Rome seemed angry when I turned up. He was adamant he didn't ask for the farm to be valued. If he didn't then why was I called out?" she asked, as she thought back to the conversation Rome and Georgina had shared that morning when she was eavesdropping on them. She had heard Rome blame Georgina for Emily turning up here but then Georgina had denied it and said her dad had been trying to give Rome a kick up the bum, whatever that was supposed to mean. Seth was silent. Just then the sheep grunted and stretched up its head. Its body stiffened and then released as it went back to panting.

"She's pushing," said Seth. He clearly wasn't going to answer Emily's question. Maybe she had been too intrusive. "Why don't you move round to her back end and take a look?"

Emily raised her eyebrows and shuffled round slowly. Then she saw something: a little greyish bud was protruding from the sheep.

"What's that bit?" Emily asked, alarmed.

"That's the lamb's nose," Seth explained, looking down at the sheep.

"Does that mean she's going to do it on her own, then?" asked Emily, hopefully.

"We've got a lot of things that could go wrong yet," Seth said, quietly. Emily watched as the sheep went tense and relaxed over and over as it tried to push out its lamb. Soon enough they could see the whole head and one other little grey thing under its chin.

"What's that bit?" Emily asked.

"It's the lamb's foot. Where's the other one?" Seth looked concerned and Emily searched his face to try and tell what situation they were in. Seth cleared his throat.

"We'll give her a few more minutes and then we might have to intervene," he said.

Emily's stomach lurched with fear. She couldn't believe she was going to have to do this. What if she did it wrong and hurt the sheep? She tried to think back to the midwife shows she had watched on TV. How different was a lamb to a baby? A few minutes passed slowly as they watched the sheep.

"Okay." Seth took hold of his crutches and moved round the back of the sheep to stand beside Emily. "We're going to have to give it some help. I think one of the legs might be stuck back so it means the shoulder could get stuck. You'll have to reach in and try and feel for the other leg."

Seth said it calmly, but Emily had never felt so utterly afraid. She didn't know what the hell she was meant to feel for. In a moment of doubt she suggested, "Why can't we just call Rome? You must have his number."

"Because Rome never answers his phone and it will take us an age to find a signal. It's a waste of time, and I think you'll be absolutely fine. I'll guide you through it." Seth sounded reassuring as Emily took some deep shaky breaths.

"Just move so you're right behind the sheep. Roll your sleeves up too, it's going to get messy." Seth kept going as Emily did what he was telling her. "Now you have to put your hand in under the head to the left and feel for the left leg. Just do it slowly and gently. You'll be fine."

Seth was patient and encouraging and Emily felt like she might actually be able to do this. What a story she'd have to tell. Maybe Rome wouldn't be so grumpy with her if she pulled this off, or out, as it were. She rolled up her sleeves and did as Seth instructed. With one last look at her chipped manicure she sighed and carefully put her hand under the lamb's head into the sheep to try and find the missing leg. It was warm and she tried not to think about it as she continued to search for the leg.

"You're doing great, can you feel it?" asked Seth encouraging. Emily shook her head.

"Maybe it's a three legged lamb?" she suggested.

"I hope not. You'll have to go a bit further because the leg is probably stuck back. You'll have to grab the leg and bring it forwards out of the sheep so she can push the lamb out. Once you've got both legs you can pull each time the sheep pushes."

Emily tried to take in all the advice as she felt for the leg. Finally she had it. She felt something slimy and leg like.

"I think I've got it." She looked up at Seth.

"That's it. Now bring it forward," he urged.

Emily pulled on the leg and felt it coming forwards. It took effort and time but she managed to get the leg free and out of the sheep. A rush of fluid came out with the leg and spread across Emily's legs, causing her to gag. She wasn't used to smells like that. She heard Seth laugh. Emily grimaced, blinking her watery eyes rapidly before looking up at Seth.

"I did it," she said. He was smiling. Emily couldn't believe she was actually doing this.

"Brilliant. Now when I tell you to, grab both front feet and pull," Seth said. Emily took another breath and grasped both the feet, waiting for Seth's command.

"Okay, go now, she's pushing." Emily pulled and the lamb inched further until its neck was out. She ignored the feeling of her warm wet jeans clinging to her legs.

"That's it, great," said Seth. "Don't be afraid to really pull; they can be tough to get out. And again now."

Emily pulled, a little harder this time. She really leant back and pulled and the lamb came further out. She had its front shoulders free.

"Perfect. Home stretch now. It should come easily," Seth encouraged. "Now!"

Emily pulled and leant back, then fell back on her bum as the lamb came free. It fell onto the straw behind its mother. Her jaw gaped as she looked at the lamb on the floor, gooey and covered with a sac-like jelly coat.

"It's still partly in the sac so you have to be quick now and rip the afterbirth away, then clear its nose like I explained to you earlier." Seth was more serious now. The mother sheep made baaing noises as Emily knelt over the lamb and pulled away the afterbirth. She grabbed its nose and let it slip through her hand as she cleared the mucus away so it could breathe. She waited. The seconds felt like hours. The anticipation made her feel physically sick.

"It's not breathing." She looked up at Seth desperately wishing he could take over. She felt so out of her depth.

"Get a blade of straw and poke it up both the lamb's nostrils," he instructed, talking fast. Emily did it without questioning the craziness. Nothing. "Rub its belly up and down fast and hard," said Seth. Emily did it but it wouldn't breath. "Okay, one last trick. Pick it up by its back legs and swing it from side to side."

Emily starred up at him. She swallowed hard. "Are you actually joking? I don't think this is the time for a laugh."

"Nope, not joking. Do it now, we're running out of time," Seth insisted.

Emily stood up and grabbed the lamb by its back legs. She raised it so its head was above the ground as she swung it from side to side. The lamb choked and sneezed, then came to life in Emily's hands. She lowered it to the ground and it lay on the straw as it took its first breaths.

"Oh my God," she shrieked.

"Shhh," said Seth, laughing. "You did amazing."

She looked from Seth to the lamb and squeaked a little with excitement as the lamb lifted its wobbly head to look around. She was so overwhelmed with relief and adrenalin that she had to hold back tears. Her fear of sheep was forgotten as she watched the small, wet lamb.

"Now pick up the lamb and just place it by its mother's head. She'll lick it off. You can make little bleating noises so the mother thinks the lamb is calling to her. It will encourage her to mother it," Seth said.

"Now you really are joking aren't you? I'm not falling for that just to have you laugh at me," Emily said.

Seth's face stayed straight. "No, I'm not joking. I won't judge your sheep impression." He smirked then.

Emily laughed as she picked up the wet, white lamb and lifted it to its mother's head.

"Baa," she said, but it came out in a splutter as she tried to hold her laughter in. Seth chuckled.

"Short little baas," he said, and then followed up with an impression. Emily baaed like a sheep and felt more embarrassed than she had since she arrived on the farm. She placed the lamb down by the mother and watched in awe as the sheep licked its baby.

"Wow," she breathed as tears pricked her eyes. "Do you think it's too late for me to retrain as a midwife?"

"You were seriously impressive. You wouldn't see many town girls on their knees behind a sheep, covered in afterbirth. You're a natural."

Emily grinned and looked down at her clothes. She was grateful she'd put the others in the wash because it looked like she'd be showering and changing once again. Just then, they turned to hear a car pull up outside the farmhouse.

"Bit late, Rome," Seth said, under his breath. Emily heard the car door shut and Seth called Rome's name. She heard footsteps on the gravel coming towards them. Rome appeared round the side of the house and jogged down to the lambing shed. He came through the gate and put his hands on his hips as he observed the scene before him. Emily watched his face. His eyebrows were raised and he looked from Seth to the sheep to her. Emily waited eagerly for a reaction.

"She did it all," Seth said. "She was amazing. It had a leg stuck. She did the whole thing and then got it breathing when it came out. It's a big one as well."

Rome raised his eyebrows. "Maybe we *have* found ourselves a farm hand."

Emily couldn't help but feel proud that she'd won Rome's approval. After all the blunders and mistakes, she had finally done something useful. She'd brought a life into the world. It made her life and the worries back home feel small. In London she worried about fitting in enough house viewings. She stressed constantly about this new promotion. She had convinced herself that she had an important job helping people find their dream home, but what could compare to this? Emily caught Rome's eye and he smiled at her. It lit up his face and showed off his dimples. She couldn't help but feel a small flutter of butterflies.

"I think it's only fair you name it since you brought it into the world," said Rome, without breaking eye contact with her. Emily had never named an animal before.

"Susie," she announced finally. Rome approached her and walked round the front of the ewe to take a look at the lamb. He pulled it down towards the mother's tummy and then helped it latch onto the teat to drink.

"Susie's a boy," Rome looked up at her.

"Oh, right." Emily thought again. "Shawn then."

"Shawn it is. The first lamb of the season. I can't believe I missed it." Rome shook his head.

The three of them spent another half hour watching the sheep and Emily went through what she had done to get it out and get it to breathe and she took great pleasure in watching Rome's facial expressions. He looked impressed.

*

Emily slipped onto the sofa after vigorously washing her hands as Rome sorted the kettle. Birdie and Tess came over to her and their wet tongues licked at her clothes, probably smelling the afterbirth. She held her hands up then gave one a light pat on the head.

"Birdie, Tess, lie down," Rome commanded and they scurried off to the fire, curling around each other on the floor like two little squirrels. Rome handed Emily a cup of tea which she gratefully accepted. He sat next to her on the sofa with his coffee. Emily felt very aware of their close proximity as she sipped her tea.

"I really appreciate what you did out there tonight," he said.

"It's fine. Seth was great; he told me exactly what to do. I enjoyed it, actually." Emily smiled to herself, sipping her tea.

"I should have been here with Seth's leg broken. It was irresponsible but I couldn't skip that dinner." Rome looked over at the fire and his two dogs.

"Dinner with your girlfriend?" Emily blurted out before she could stop herself. "Sorry, that was rude. I didn't mean to pry."

"No, it's fine." Rome stood up. She'd lost his attention again. "I'd better get off to bed," he said. "I'll be getting up early to check on the lamb."

He made to walk away seeming to forget about his coffee.

"What time will you be getting up?" Emily asked.

"Probably about half four or five. I don't set an alarm. I just wake up," he said. Emily nodded. Rome gave a quick, tight-lipped smile and went upstairs. Emily grabbed her clothes from the wash and hung them on the clothes horse in front of the dwindling fire. She popped a few logs on moving carefully around Birdie and Tess.

Emily ran upstairs and took another quick shower with her hair tied up and then slumped down in bed. Tiredness gripped her. Her mind was full of a million and one things: the lamb, Mark, Rome. She caught herself. Why did she have Rome on her mind?

Rome

Rome woke up and stretched full length. He threw back the duvet and climbed out of bed. There was still a hazy darkness lingering the other side of the window, but he knew that, in an hour, the sun would begin to rise. The animals were always awake and hungry before the sun was up which meant Rome had to be up and out to feed them.

Rome threw on his work clothes from the day before and quietly went downstairs, careful not to wake Emily. He was greeted by Birdie and Tess, who sprang at him with tails wagging, tongues licking. "Good girls," he said. As he walked through the living room towards the kettle he couldn't help but notice a pair of frilly knickers hanging from his clothes horse. Rome yawned as the kettle boiled and raked a hand through his unruly hair. He made and downed a coffee then headed for the back door.

"Wait." A quiet voice from behind stopped him.

He turned around. Emily was stood there with a blanket wrapped around her. He watched her shuffle sideways to the clothes horse. She quickly swiped her knickers away and cleared her throat. Rome suppressed a smirk.

"I'll get dressed and come with you," she said, grabbing the rest of her clothes. Rome was a little taken aback, having had no idea town girls could be this keen to farm. He couldn't possibly say no, though, not when she had gotten up in the early hours and was insisting on helping with his work.

"I'll wait here." He gave her a quick smile and she went off upstairs.

Two minutes later she was back, dressed in the shirt and jeans he'd given her on the first day. Her blond hair was up in a ponytail. She wasn't wearing makeup but still looked undeniably pretty. He looked away quickly and made for the back door. She followed him and they went out into the dark morning. Rome strode across the yard, towards his tractor, and he heard Emily catching up behind him. He climbed up into the cab and left the door open so she could climb in after him.

"I'll drive this time, shall I?" Rome teased. He saw her smile as she climbed up into the little passenger seat next to him. He reached across her to shut the heavy tractor door, accidently brushing his sleeve across her chest as he drew his arm back. He kept his eyes forward and turned on the tractor's headlights.

They picked up a bale on the forks from the stack on their way down to the lambing shed. Rome stole a glance at Emily to see her eagerly looking forwards into the shed to catch sight of her lamb. He lowered the hay bale down into the hay ring and the sheep surrounded it, pulling bits off and munching.

"Check that lamb of yours, shall we?" Rome said. Emily nodded and they climbed down from the tractor cab to enter the barn. Rome pulled off an arm full of hay for the mother ewe as they approached her pen. He saw Emily go over, blissfully unaffected by the other sheep milling around her as she knelt down beside the hurdle pen and looked in at the lamb.

Rome put the hay down for the mother sheep, who chewed at it. The lamb was on its feet, suckling.

"Looks strong and healthy," Rome said.

Emily looked up at him.

"I still can't believe I pulled him out."

"You did well," he said. "At least something good came out of your wasted trip."

He realised he probably owed Emily a bigger apology for the fact that her time had been wasted driving all the way to Devon. He'd been too angry thinking about why she was here to consider how much of an inconvenience it must be for her.

"I wouldn't say my time was wasted," Emily said. "Look at Shawn," she pointed to the lamb, "I've never gotten to do anything like this before, and even though it was the most nerve-wracking thing I've ever done, I'd probably do it again if I had to. I'm an expert tractor driver now, too."

Rome watched her face crease into happiness, her dimples showing, her eyes shining with joy. He couldn't help but feel a cutting sadness at that. It was impossible not to think of *her* when he watched Emily. They were too similar. He leant over the hurdle and gave the lamb a little scratch on the bum. It waggled its tail, while the mother ewe stamped her foot.

"We'd better get on," said Rome. Emily rose from the floor and followed him across the lambing shed. Rome looked around to check for any more that might have been born in the night or that looked close. It all looked fine for now. They got back in the tractor and sorted the cows with some silage. Emily made a face at the smell but she didn't seem too bothered. They put in a round straw bale and jumped out. Rome approached the gate to go in.

"We're not going in there, are we?" Emily took a step back. "What are you going in for?"

"We need to bed them up." Rome looked at Emily's confused expression. "You know? Spread the straw around." Rome untied the gate to go in. "They won't hurt you, I raised them on the bucket."

He watched Emily's brow crease.

"I don't do farm speak," she said.

"I've fed them and raised them since they were calves. There are no crazies in here." Rome watched her approach the gate. She looked at him warily.

"You can wait in the tractor if you really want," he said. Emily looked at the cows and sighed.

"Let's just do it," she said. "At least I'll die doing something useful."

She stepped through the gate and Rome watched as her eyes widened. She visibly swallowed.

"You won't die, stupid," he said, with a laugh, as he followed her in. After cutting the net wrap off, Rome braced his hands on the round bale.

"Help me push?" he raised his eyebrows at her. She frowned slightly and walked over, not taking her eyes off the cows for a second.

"So we just roll it around?" she asked.

"Yep."

Emily placed her hands on the bale next to him and they began to push it around the barn. It unravelled, leaving a trail of straw behind them. They built up momentum and Emily laughed. Rome liked that. He couldn't deny having her around had cheered him up. He found himself smiling when he was trying his best not to.

The cows jumped behind them and ran, shaking their heads from side to side. Emily squealed and hunched her body up, arms over her face. Rome couldn't help but let a laugh escape.

"They're just excited. They love being bedded up. They want to play," he explained. He saw Emily relax a little but kept her back to the bale, watching the cows warily.

"We're almost done. Don't stop now," he encouraged her. They finished off the bale and left the shed, climbing back into the tractor. The sun was coming up now, peeking above the hills in the valley and illuminating the farm.

"Looks like it'll be a warm day today," he said, as they parked the tractor. "It's been nice for April." They walked across the yard. "There's just the horse to feed and then we'll go in and get some breakfast and let the dogs out."

"You have a horse?" Emily's face lit up.

"Are you not scared of horses then?"

"I've never touched one but I think I'll like them."

They reached the stable. Rome patted the big, bay horse as it leaned its head out to greet them.

"This is Bramley," he said. Emily smiled as she gingerly reached forward to touch the horse's face. She snatched her hand back as Bramley snorted. Rome grabbed a few wedges of hay from the empty stable next to Bramley and dropped them over his door.

"You can groom him if you want." Rome went to the tack room to get some brushes and offered one to Emily.

"Aren't you going to tie him up first?" she asked, nervously.

"No. You'll be fine. He's the laziest thing, not a bad bone in his body. He's been retired for a few years now. Just plods around the valley all summer." Rome went in and Emily followed, hovering at the door. He started to brush the tall horse from his neck down to his back and, soon enough, Emily followed him in and was brushing him too, keeping her feet a firm distance away from his hooves.

"Why is he retired? Is he old?" Emily asked. Rome was caught off guard with the question. Just then he felt his phone vibrate in his pocket. Relieved, he pulled it out and flipped it up to answer it.

"Hello? Yep. All right mate, thanks. Bye." Rome snapped the phone shut and buried it back in his pocket.

"That was Darren," Rome said. "Looks like the part for your car might not be in for a few days. He said he doesn't really stock parts for cars like yours. He's used to old battered trucks and tractors."

"I can't have time off work and I've already outstayed my welcome. I'll see if I can get a taxi back today. I'll just have to come and collect my car when it's done," Emily said.

"I said I could give you a lift," Rome reminded her.

"I don't want to be any trouble," Emily said. "You have your sheep to look after and I really don't mind getting a cab."

"Seth can keep an ear out for the sheep while I'm gone. How far is it back to London? A few hours?" Rome asked.

"Three if the traffic is good," said Emily. Rome knew he shouldn't really leave his flock for that long but if the worst came to the worst Seth could hobble around the farm, get some signal and call the vet. Usually they had their lambs without much difficulty anyway. He knew it was irresponsible but he really wanted to give Emily a lift home to make it up to her.

In the short few days Emily had been here Rome had felt strangely happy for the first time in a long time.

In two short days she'd proven her worth on the farm, she'd shown such keenness and Rome liked that about her. Was it good she invoked memories of *her* in him or should he be staying as far away as possible? He didn't know. Then again, it was only a lift home.

"No, I can take you," Rome insisted, making up his mind. Emily smiled.

"Thank you."

"Right, shall we go and get something to eat? Then we can take you back if you'd like. I've got a few other bits to do today. Splitting logs and that, so we'll get you back before I have to start that." Rome patted Bramley on the neck and left the stable chucking his brush back through the tack room door.

Emily

An hour later, after Emily had hungrily finished off the fry-up Rome had made for her completely unfazed by the amount of calories it contained, she was standing over Shawn's hurdle pen, saying goodbye to the little lamb she'd helped into the world. She lifted her phone to take a picture, realising at the same time that she hadn't missed the constant calls, texts and social media drama as much as she had thought she would. It had been like a holiday here; a slightly stressful one, but a break from her busy life nonetheless. She would miss it.

Emily left the sheep pen and tied the gate behind her, deciding she would go and say goodbye to Seth.

Emily walked past the back of the wild farmhouse garden and over to the little cottage. She knocked on the door. Seth answered and greeted her with a smile.

"Not another sheep?" he asked.

"No," Emily replied. "I just came to say goodbye. Rome is going to give me a lift home. It was nice to meet you though."

"It was nice to meet you too. You were a big help last night. Rome might seem a bit grumpy and he might not thank you but I know he'll be grateful inside."

Emily looked down and smiled. Rome was a bit of a mystery to her but then, she didn't know him well enough to make assumptions about his personality. Emily looked up at Seth.

"I'd better get going, it's a long trip home."

"Bye," he said.

Emily heard the cottage door shut behind her as she turned to leave. As she walked past the farmhouse garden she saw a little gate nestled deep in an overgrown hedgerow which she hadn't noticed before. She walked over and peered through the little gap in the hedge. There was greenery the other side, but also a flash of pink. She couldn't see well enough through the coiled hedge in front of her. Curiosity tugged at her.

She peeked back at the cottage and over to the farmhouse, then approached the gate. Emily undid the rusty, brown latch and pushed. The gate was entangled closed with brambles. She pushed harder and the brambles ripped and tore away from the gate as she barged her way in.

The gate fell open. Dandelion seeds floated past and the sight before her was revealed. Rows of spindly trees were blanketed with pink blossoms. It was gorgeous. There must have been hundreds, all fenced in with a huge green hedge. A paddock of blossom trees stood there, hidden from the valley and the bad weather. The sun shone a hazy glow over a beautiful scene and Emily took it all in, listening to the birds chirping all around her. It was like a secret garden. It was so hidden, a tranquil haven like something out of a movie.

Emily recognised the apple trees for what they were then. It was a big orchard. Why was it so overgrown and neglected, though? The grass was long and wispy. Among it was vibrant purple vetch tangled with bright pink clover. Tall white cow parsley dotted the hedgerows. Emily didn't know a lot about countryside plants but she'd learnt a bit from watching *Escape to the Country*.

The trees had brambles growing around their trunks. The hedge was out of control and unkempt. A weeping willow cascaded in tendrils in one corner. The beauty was being eaten by thorns but Emily could picture how pretty it could be if someone just tended to it. Becoming suddenly conscious she was snooping she turned to leave, and noticed a little sign on the gate. It was so faded she could barely read it: *Bramblewood cider orchards*. Emily tugged the gate shut behind her and made her way back to the house to gather up her things. The secret orchard lingered in her thoughts as she opened the back door to the farmhouse.

Rome was in the living room, slouched on the sofa with his eyes closed, a dog either side of him with their soft heads on his lap. There was a coffee cup perched precariously on his knee, the handle resting on his pinkie. His head was tilted back. His chest rose and fell gently and Emily watched him for a few seconds as he slept silently and peacefully. His blue, faded hoody had a torn kangaroo pouch. His muddy jeans were frayed at the bottom. His dark hair sprawled over his forehead and curled before it reached his eyebrows. He looked suddenly younger than usual. Maybe it was because he wasn't frowning, just blissfully asleep. Feeling embarrassed, she tore her eyes away, creeping past him and up the stairs to get her things.

Emily was down in the kitchen five minutes later and stood in front of Rome, who was still fast asleep. She had to get going but it felt awkward to wake him.

"Rome," she said, quietly enough not to startle him. There was no reaction.

"Rome," she said, louder. The dogs awoke and wagged at Emily. One of them jumped down off the sofa, upsetting the mug on Rome's knee. It tumbled to the ground and hit the floor, causing the other dog to leap up and jump down. This woke Rome up and he was evidently startled to see Emily standing over him. He looked a little dazed as he sat up and noticed the coffee mug on the floor. Emily bent down to grab it just as Rome did and they banged heads.

"Sorry," they both said, at the same time.

Emily let out an awkward laugh as Rome picked the cup up and offered out his hand to Emily which she took. Rome helped her to her feet and they stood there like the first time they had met. Emily didn't let go. She wasn't sure why but he wasn't letting go either. When she looked at him he was already looking at her. She was so aware of her hand in his larger one, the way it enclosed hers. Then the trance was broken as he slipped his hand away and left hers dangling. He walked away like there'd been no unspoken moment, no electricity. She watched as he went over to the sink and submerged his cup. Did he drink anything other than coffee?

"Ready?" he asked. Emily was still standing in the same spot, catching her breath, dazed from his touch.

"Sure." She cleared her throat and picked up her handbag. She bent to scratch both dogs behind the ears. "Bye girls."

*

Emily gazed out the window at the fast moving scenery as they drove down the motorway in Rome's old Landrover. Her phone was on the dashboard, acting as a sat nav.

"How will you get home without a sat nav?" she asked, wondering how anyone could find their way on the three-hour journey.

"I've got a map," he said, keeping his eyes on the road ahead. Emily nodded. They were an hour or so into their journey and it had mostly been silence, apart from the radio. Emily looked out of the window again briefly before turning to him.

"I saw an orchard today when I was saying goodbye to Seth. I saw it through the little gate. It's all overgrown. How come?" Emily asked. She saw Rome's jaw tighten. He looked out the window and then back to the road. She saw his knuckles whiten on the steering wheel but to her shock he didn't reply. Had he not heard her?

"Rome?"

"I can't talk right now, I'm concentrating," he said. They had miles left on this motorway. The sat nav hadn't peeped for about ten minutes. The silence was back and now it was tinged with awkwardness.

After three gruelling hours on the road they finally pulled up outside Emily's apartment on the outskirts of London. Rome's Landrover looked out of place against the smart blocks of flats. Emily hoped Mark wouldn't be home. He was usually out on a Sunday playing golf with his friends.

Emily stretched before gathering up her handbag, phone and the carrier bag on the floor that had her muddy heels in. She was wearing the wellies Rome had lent her. She looked up at the block of flats and then at Rome. He looked at her. They both began to speak at the same time.

"Sorry, you go," said Emily.

"I just wanted to say, sorry you got called to my place for nothing. I hope you won't get in trouble with your boss."

Emily was certain she wouldn't.

Rome kept going. "And I wanted to say thanks for your help."

"I'm sure I only got in the way," Emily said.

"You really didn't." Rome looked down for a second and Emily waited for him to speak. "I guess I'll call you when your car is fixed."

"You don't have my number."

Rome reached into his jeans pocket and took his phone out. He handed it to her. She looked at the little phone, unsure if she even knew how to use it. She flipped it up and a few little husks of straw fell onto her lap. She put in her number and saved it. Emily couldn't help but notice Georgina's name beneath hers. Rome didn't have many contacts. Most were women though. Helen, Mandy. What was she doing? She shouldn't be looking. She quickly handed him the phone back.

"I've saved it under Emily Rogers."

"I'll miss having you around," he replied, looking at her. Emily knew she should get out of the car now but she couldn't help the fact that she didn't want to. They didn't break eye contact for what felt like a while and neither of them spoke until Emily shattered the silence.

"Well, thanks for the lift, I'm really grateful." As she went for the door handle she wanted him to stop her. It was crazy. She had only known him two days, he had a girlfriend, she had Mark, and the very sight of her seemed to make him grumpy sometimes. Even so, she couldn't help the way she felt.

Rome didn't stop Emily, though, so, while it pained her to get of the car, she did. She shut the door with one last smile. Was it wrong that she felt deflated as he glanced at her through the window, put his Landrover in gear and drove away?

Rome

Rome sat at the kitchen table that night, Irish whisky in front of him. He drank from the bottle. He'd got home and lambed another ewe, split logs, fed the cattle. Emily had been on his mind the whole time. It had been strange saying goodbye to her. For a split second the thought of what it might be like to kiss her had galloped through his mind. He'd thought about Georgina and it banished the crazy image.

He took another gulp of whisky. Seth was sitting on the sofa with Rome's dogs. They'd just ordered a take away. They were going to take turns tonight going out to check on the ewes. Rome was aware Seth was looking at him as he gulped from the bottle.

"Steady on, mate. You need to be able to stand tonight if a ewe goes," Seth said, laughing, but Rome noticed his sideways glance of concern.

"I've got it," Rome reassured him.

"What is it? Georgina? Helen? Emily maybe?" Seth asked. Rome took another hard gulp at the mention of the three main women on his mind.

"Women, ay?" said Rome, looking over to where Seth sat on the sofa. "It's fine Seth, stop worrying. I've got it under control."

He just wanted to numb everything for a while, even just for the night. There was a knock at the door.

"Finally some food." Rome stood up. He was lightheaded enough that he floated to the back door, knocking into the kitchen door frame with his shoulder. As he hauled the door open he was almost disappointed to see Georgina.

"Rome, you didn't answer my calls." Her voice was shrill against the backdrop of the whisky. He needed her to lower it.

"Shhh Georgina, what is it?" Rome slurred.

"Have you been drinking?" Her brow furrowed into a disapproving glower. She always looked angry with her tight ponytail and green eyes, which cut through him as they stared. Her arms were crossed tightly over her chest. Rome held up his whisky bottle, which he planned on having attached to his hand for the rest of the evening.

"Yep, I've had a little one. Problem?" he asked. "What are you here for, Georgina? Is it to debt collect for daddy or to see me?" she scowled at him and snatched his bottle of whisky away just as he went to take another sip.

"I don't like you drunk," she snapped.

"Give that back." Rome needed it. She tipped it up and started to pour it out. Rome reached for it and stumbled forward. Georgina easily dodged him and held the bottle out of reach.

"Look at the state of you," she said. "If you want to keep me, Rome, then you need to stop this. You won't get another chance." She poured out the rest of the bottle and shook it to eliminate the last drops.

"That was expensive whisky," he said.

"You have other things to spend your money on," Georgina scolded. "Daddy won't wait forever. You're racking up a debt so you better start sorting your shit out."

Rome just wanted her to leave.

"You can forget seeing me tonight in this state. I'll see you in the week, I'm going away for a few days to a horse competition."

Rome didn't answer; he was trying to think about where he'd put the other bottle. He knew he had more somewhere.

"Are you going to say anything?" Georgina asked, as she stared at him.

He looked down at her. It made him dizzy.

"Have a good time," he managed.

She handed him the empty bottle. "Are you going to kiss me goodbye?"

He wasn't planning on it but he couldn't really refuse. He kissed her briefly then turned to go back inside.

"Last chance, Rome," she called after him, still sounding angry.

He shut the door hard and went back into the kitchen.

"It wasn't the pizza," he called to Seth.

"Obviously," Seth replied, coming into the kitchen. Rome rummaged in the cupboards for another bottle.

"What are you looking for?" Seth asked.

"She tipped my drink away," he said, as he continued rummaging.

"It's probably for the best," said Seth.

No. Rome needed a little more.

"You need to be careful. She won't give you endless chances," Seth warned.

Rome turned to look at him.

"Can't *you* just date her instead?"

"Don't be ridiculous," said Seth.

Rome finally found his bottle. He opened the top and swigged. "There you are, you little bugger."

Emily

As Emily woke up she took a moment to glance around the room. It was the morning after Rome had driven her home and she was back in her own bed at her and Mark's apartment. Mark wasn't there, hadn't been all night. She hadn't bothered to text to ask where he was. She suspected he was occupied with something much more interesting than her.

Feeling frustrated Emily put on black tights, a black pencil skirt and a white button-down top finished off with a black blazer. She hadn't slept well last night. The noise of the traffic outside had her tossing and turning. It was only then that she had realised how silent Bramblewood Farm had been.

Emily put her hair up in a neat bun and applied makeup. She walked out of the en-suite bathroom through to the bedroom to get her handbag and phone. She spotted Rome's shirt on the floor; the one she had borrowed. She took a deep breath and pushed Rome to the back of her mind. She was back in the real world now. Whatever weird connection she felt with him was over and she had to get on and go to work.

Emily kicked the shirt under the bed with her heel. She'd deal with it later. She had planned on getting a lift into work with Mark but since he wasn't here she called a cab. A honk outside prompted her to rush through the kitchen and into the lift to take her downstairs to her waiting taxi.

Emily walked through the door of the estate agents and was immediately hit with the familiar synthetic plastic office smell. As she made her way to her office, she decided she preferred the natural smell of the farm. She made a few greetings and hellos on the way.

Emily dumped her handbag on her desk and turned on her computer. She would go straight to the boss's office and explain the mishap at the farm so they could take the property off their list of places to be valued.

Emily approached Mark's office. *Mark Johnson*, read the silver plaque on the door. Pushing the door open she walked straight in.

Emily's stomach hit the floor as she took in the scene before her. There she saw Mark at his desk, obscured by the woman who was *on* his desk. Her long legs were either side of him. Her head was bent and they were locked in a kiss.

Mark scrabbled backwards on his office chair when he heard the door go. His face was a picture when he saw Emily standing there. His jaw gapped open and closed like a fish's. The woman slid down from the desk and turned to face Emily. Rage built inside her.

"You didn't even shut the blind. Classy Mark, real classy," said Emily, looking behind them at the bustling street. "Do you think we could talk in private, Sophie?"

Emily gave her colleague a smile dripping with venom. Sophie bolted from the room, keeping her head low. Two guesses as to who was going to get the big promotion, Emily thought. Without turning,

Emily slammed the door behind her and locked eyes with Mark, arms crossed firmly over her chest.

"I didn't think you'd be back yet," Mark said. She stared at him bitterly, finding his stupid slicked-back hair even more annoying now.

"Oh, sorry Mark," Emily said, "shall I call Sophie back? You don't have to stop on my account." Things started to slot into place in her head. "You sent me off to that job on the farm when you knew damn well I'd never even valued rural property before. There are plenty more experienced people in the office. You know I hate driving and it's a three hour bloody trek. You wanted me out the way."

Emily bubbled with anger. Mark hadn't even apologised yet. In fact, Emily wasn't even sure if he looked the slightest bit sorry, but then, his face had always had an unsettlingly smug look about it.

"It just happened, I didn't plan it." Mark threw his hands up. Emily knew better than to stand there listening to his lies. She already knew she was done so what was the point in dragging it out?

"Screw you, Mark. I quit." She turned and opened the door to leave.

"Oh yeah? And who do you think will take you without a reference after a six-year position?" Mark retorted.

"Good luck paying my half of the rent, Mark." Emily didn't look back as she shut the door firmly behind her. She retrieved her handbag and walked straight out the office flipping Sophie off on the way.

Beneath the initial blinding fury Emily began to feel a small hint of relief. Mark had screwed her over too many times. He would never get the chance again. Emily deserved better and she knew it. More than anything, she felt stupid. Stupid she had stayed so long through all of his lies and deceit, all of the nights he didn't come home, all of the times he didn't show up. Now, he had made her look like an idiot in her work place. They probably all knew what Mark was up to. People she called her friends hadn't bothered to tell her. She had thought her and *Sophie* were friends despite their battle for the promotion. Oh, how wrong she was.

As Emily hiked brusquely down the street the severity of the situation began to dawn on her. She was unemployed and homeless. That'd teach her for dating her boss. Four years of her life with him utterly wasted and down the drain. She had been swept up in his undeniable charm, naively thinking she would 'be the one that changed him' and pull him out of his notorious bachelor ways. She wouldn't let herself be blinded like that again.

Emily wracked her brains for a place she might be able to stay. Her dad lived in America, and she hadn't seen him in years. They rarely even spoke. Her mum lived eight hours across the country and quite frankly Emily didn't relish the idea of sharing a house with her again. They didn't exactly see eye to eye.

She was living Mark's life now. Her friends were his friends, her home was his home. She had lost her identity to him and now she was paying the price but she was free and that was what mattered. Still, was freedom a good thing when you were homeless? She had about ten hours to brainstorm before Mark was home from work. *If* he came home that was.

Emily walked all the way back to the flat and an hour later she was in her bedroom, flinging clothes into a giant suitcase. She was sweating and flustered as she marched round the flat, gathering up the essentials. He could send the rest to her, wherever that might be. All she wanted now was to be out of his life. She packed her bathroom things as she thought about places she might be able to stay. She really didn't have a single friend who wasn't also Mark's. Why had she let it go on so long? She had ignorantly brushed away the signs. She had even thought that he might propose soon. So stupid. He was immature, self-centred and narcissistic and she shouldn't have given him so long to get his priorities straight.

Emily slammed her suitcase shut and zipped it. She didn't even know how long she was packing for. She had savings but she didn't want to squander them on a hotel. She would have to find another a job.

It was a few hours later as Emily was finishing a glass of Mark's extortionately expensive wine which he'd been saving, each sip tainted with the sweet hint of revenge, when she got a call. It was an unknown number. She promptly hung up. Probably Mark using someone else's phone to get at her. He would definitely do something like that. The phone rang again a minute later. This time she answered it feeling exasperated.

"What do you want Mark?" she said into the phone.

"This is Rome Buckley, do I have the wrong number?" the voice on the other end of the line said.

"Oh my God! Rome. I'm so sorry. I thought you were someone else." She felt a mixture of things. Embarrassment for one, but the rest was too complex to pick apart.

"I just called to let you know that Darren said the part came today. It was quicker than he thought. He's going to fix your car this afternoon, so it should be ready to collect tonight," Rome said.

"That's great, thank you." It meant a long cab ride out to the farm but at least she would have her car and she wouldn't be stuck.

"So, who's Mark? You're lucky I called again. I never call twice," said Rome.

"My ex," replied Emily, thankful to finally be able to call him that.

"I see," Rome sounded a little uncomfortable. "I can get Darren to drop your car off to the farm so you know where you're going, if you want."

Something in Emily lit up at the thought of seeing him again.

"That would be great, thank you. I'll see you at some point this afternoon."

"Sure. See you then," said Rome, and the line went dead.

*

Emily had bundled her giant suitcase, duffle bag and handbag into the taxi about three and a half hours ago and now they were inching their way up the narrow country lane towards the farm track. She had grabbed Rome's shirt out from under the bed and put it on before she left, not really knowing why. It was just comfy and she wanted to be comfy right now. She'd also worn the wellies which she'd gone home in, not eager to ruin another pair of heels. The taxi stopped at the entrance to the farm. The long, rutted track stretched out ahead of them.

"You'll have to get out here, love. I won't make it down that lane," the old driver said.

"Yeah, I've been *there*," said Emily, as she got out and grabbed her suit case and duffle bag. She paid the driver and he reversed back down the lane.

The sun hung low in the sky as Emily shifted her duffle bag up on to her back. With her handbag over one shoulder and her suitcase in hand she began the long trek all the way down the farm track.

By the time Emily reached the farmyard she was wiping her brow and fighting to catch her breath. She was exhausted from the long journey and the hike to the farm. Emily fiddled with the garden gate, struggled up to the front door and slid off her duffle bag with an audible sigh. She knocked, feeling a little nervous. When Rome answered, he had a dark green faded hoody on, with muddy jeans, scruffy hair and a coffee cup in his hand.

"Bloody hell, how long are you staying for this time?"

That's when it happened. She couldn't say why but she couldn't do anything to stop it. Her eyes brimmed with tears and she stood on his doorstep, crying. Everything had built up and now it was coming out. The stress of having her whole life change in the last five hours suddenly hit her. Rome put his mug down and without hesitating he wrapped his arms around her. Emily was shocked at first, but she found herself hugging him back. She didn't know how long they stayed like that but she savoured the feeling of his arms around her, pressing into her back. He made her feel small as he encased her. She could smell his skin, the familiar farmyard smells mixed with apples and coffee and felt the heat of him through her shirt. She couldn't remember the last time she and Mark had hugged like that. In fact, she didn't know if they ever had, in the four years they'd been together. She had only known this man three or four days. When he drew back she felt as though she might fall. He smiled gently at her, then grabbed her duffle bag and suitcase and took them inside. Emily stared after him.

"Rome?" she called from the doorway. "I'm going to need those."

He appeared from the kitchen.

"You mean you're not staying?"

"No. I'm just here to collect my car."

"Why have you packed your life up then?" he frowned.

"I broke up with my partner. I moved out of our flat," she licked her dry lips.

"Why don't you come in for a minute?" He stepped aside to invite her in and went through to the kitchen. She bent to stroke the dogs and they nestled their faces into her.

"Hello girls." Emily was overwhelmingly surprised that Rome would have accepted her into his home with all of her bags and not even questioned it. He hadn't paused or hesitated as he'd grabbed her bags and taken them in. Emily didn't know if he was a little mad or just kinder than she had first thought.

Emily sat down at the kitchen table and Rome sat opposite her. She watched as he lowered himself into the chair and sighed heavily.

"So, when you said you thought I was your ex on the phone. You mean this recent ex," Rome said. Emily nodded.

"What happened?" he asked looking at her.

Emily cleared her throat and gathered herself before she explained. "He cheated on me. I walked in on him with another woman who I thought was my friend. I'm certain it's not the first time."

Rome's eyebrows rose and he rubbed the stubble along his jawline.

"What mad man would cheat on you?"

Emily felt her cheeks flush.

"That's not the whole story." Emily forced down a pang of shame as she admitted the rest. "He was also my boss. So, I walked out the office this morning and quit my job. I've been there six years. I started there when I was nineteen. Mark was my first real relationship. We live together. *Lived* together. So now I have nowhere to live either."

Rome nodded slowly as he took it in.

"So you need a job?" he said, putting his hands behind his head and leaning back. "And a home?"

"I guess so, but I haven't really thought that far ahead yet," admitted Emily.

"So where were you heading with all that stuff?" he asked.

"I don't know. My mum is the other end of the country. There, I guess. Although honestly, the last thing I want to do is drive for eight hours and stay with her. All my friends are Mark's friends so I don't really have anyone to turn to."

Rome was silent for a while.

"Well, I know farming isn't really your scene but you're clearly a natural. Seth and I still need a hand on the farm while his leg is getting better. That'll take six weeks. Why don't you just stay?" He looked up at her. Emily didn't know what to say. Rome backtracked quickly. "Sorry, that's too forward of me. We don't even know each other. You don't want to work on a farm."

Rome looked down and picked at the kitchen table.

"Actually I love Bramblewood Farm. I wasn't sure at first but after I delivered Shawn it dawned on me how rewarding your work is. But I feel like I would get in the way. You're giving me a job because you feel sorry for me," Emily said.

"Absolutely not," Rome said. "I've got enough on my plate. I don't need to deal with any time wasters. You'd be a massive help. The only thing is it would actually be unpaid at the moment. The job was work for your keep. Seth was going to move in here with me and we were going to give the newbie the cottage so they could have their own place. I know it's a bit of a joke but honestly we're struggling at the moment."

Emily didn't know what the right decision was. She had nowhere to go, it was true. She had savings. She loved the farm. She'd rather not live with her overbearing, crazy mother and the thought of having to drive for eight whole hours sent cold shivers down her spine. In fact, the more she thought about it, the more impossible it seemed.

"I'll do it then." She couldn't believe she'd agreed. She couldn't believe what lay ahead of her. Mark had sent her away so he could cheat. Her old life had been ruined because of him but he'd unintentionally shoved her straight in the path of a whole new, exciting experience. Silver linings.

"I'll tell Seth to get packing then," Rome said.

"I can always just stay here. Unless you *wanted* to live with Seth. I already have all my things here. I'm not fussed about having my own space."

"As long as you're happy with that."

Emily nodded.

"Better go and unpack then hadn't you before we have to feed the cows."

*

Emily lay in bed that night exhausted to the bone from the day's madness. Mark hadn't even bothered to call her. She expected nothing less from him. He only cared about himself and whether he was happy or not. Emily had gone out and seen her lamb and a few new ones that had arrived. She and Rome had fed the cows and Emily had been braver this time when they pushed the bale around. She had carried some wood in and Rome had taught her how to light the fire. They had talked about how they would work together to get the jobs done and had agreed to take turns cooking dinner. Emily decided she was going to have to walk up the valley to find some signal and google some recipes since she didn't normally cook.

Rome

Rome watched as Emily sat on the rug in the living room feeding the newest lamb with a bottle. A ewe had given birth to twins but the mother only had enough milk for one so Rome had decided to orphan it. Emily was more than keen to take it indoors and look after it. She looked up at him and smiled as the lamb drank. He was surprised by how fast she had picked everything up. She had been there for three days and they were making a good team. They had a routine going. He was teaching her more and more, and she was much better at driving the tractor now.

Rome tugged his eyes away from Emily when the back door opened. Only Georgina didn't knock. Rome felt nerves prickle his stomach. He hadn't told Georgina about Emily moving in yet. He wasn't sure how she'd react. She appeared in the doorway of the kitchen and he saw her gaze move straight to Emily on the rug. Georgina looked at him, her expression stern.

"Shall we talk outside?" she said, her voice uneven. Rome cleared his throat and raised a hand towards the door. He followed her out.

"Would you like to explain to me why that woman is still living in your house?" Georgina crossed her arms tightly over her chest. Her eyes pierced him.

"You know I needed help, Georgina. Emily is actually good at this and I really need her around right now. It just so happens she has nowhere to live at the

~ 117 ~

moment either so it's benefitting us both," Rome explained calmly.

"Benefiting you to be able to look at her all day, you mean."

"Georgina, she has just come out of a four-year relationship. I highly doubt she's looking to hook up right now and I'm with you. You don't need to be angry. If I wanted her I'd be with her wouldn't I?"

"Oh because you can just have any woman you desire," she said, shaking her head.

"I didn't mean it like that–"

She cut him off. "You should have spoken to me before you invited another woman to live with you. You've crossed the line, Rome."

"I need the help desperately, Georgina. I don't see you dropping your horses and rushing to help me. And anyway, it was your dad that sent her in the first place," he said, arms crossed. She shook her head. He could see she was fuming. He shouldn't have taken the argument this far. She'd use it against him for months.

"He didn't send her so you could live together. I want her out," she said, sternly.

"I can't do that," said Rome, simply, unwilling to lose Emily's help on the farm.

"You could have found someone else," she pointed out. "You didn't have to pick her. Can she even farm? I bet she's never touched an animal in her life."

"Actually she's good at it and there's not many people who will work for free I'm afraid," Rome said. "She's cooking dinner tonight; why don't you stay? You can meet her and you'll see there's nothing to worry about."

Rome just wanted this drama to be over.

"Oh I *bet* she's cooking for you," she scowled.

"We're taking turns, Georgina," said Rome. "I really don't have time to cook what with having to be around the sheep full time. You're being childish. Just stay. I know you're dying to size her up anyway."

"I'm not jealous, Rome," she scoffed.

"You could have fooled me. Just stay, Georgina. Really. If you can honestly tell me you think the woman is soft on me afterwards then I'll kick her out."

"Fine I'll stay. Just for dinner. What is it anyway?" she asked, still moody.

"Roast," Rome replied.

"She's going all out, is she?"

"Stop it Georgina. Why don't you come and feed the cows with me while she finishes the dinner?"

"Fine."

Rome went back inside and saw Emily by the stove, fiddling with the oven knob. The lamb was lying down with the dogs over on the lounge rug.

"I'm just off to do the animals with Georgina. Do you think there'd be enough dinner if she stays?" he said. Emily looked over and smiled.

"Yes, there's plenty. I'm not sure how it will turn out. I haven't really done this before," she said.

"Can't be that bad if it smells good," he said, and then left swiftly before he could give Georgina another reason to shout at him.

Emily

Emily pulled out a tray of roast potatoes and shuffled them around, then stuck them back in the oven. She went to the carrier bag on the counter top, filled with things she had bought from the village earlier. Her BMW was all the way down at the end of the farm track, tucked into the gateway. She had to walk the length of the track if she wanted to go anywhere.

Emily took out the bag of cooking apples and flour. She had looked up some countryside cooking recipes and decided that farmers ate roast dinner and apple crumble, neither of which she had made before. Still, it couldn't be as hard as lambing a sheep. She found a peeler and began to peel the apples. Emily sliced them up and laid them in the bottom of a pie dish she had found in the back of the cupboard then set to work on the crumble topping. She rubbed in the flour and butter and a few other ingredients then sprinkled it over the apples. She finished it off with a dusting of cinnamon and then put it on the side to go in the oven later.

Emily grabbed four plates and took the beef and potatoes out of the oven. She turned off the veg, which was steaming, and then she dished up the food onto the plates. She made a jug of gravy and then placed the apple crumble in the oven just as the back door went and Seth followed by Georgina and Rome came through to the kitchen.

"Oh, look at that," said Seth, his eyes lighting up. "It was worth breaking my leg just for this."

He hobbled over to the table.

"You won't be saying that once you've tasted it," said Emily, carrying the plates over to the table.

"Rubbish," said Seth.

Rome was smiling, but Georgina's face was stern and pinched as she took a seat. Georgina and Rome sat on one side and Emily and Seth the other.

"Thanks for this, Emily," Rome said, as he drowned his dinner in gravy.

"It's fine, really," Emily replied.

Georgina hadn't said a word yet as Emily watched her spear a piece of broccoli. They were silent for a while as they all ate. Emily had to admit to herself she'd done a good job. It was nice; she wasn't used to home cooked food. Seth and Rome spoke across the table about the sheep and Rome was telling Seth about an awkward one he and Emily had lambed earlier that day.

"So, Emily, what happened with your estate agent job?" asked Georgina.

The question took Emily by surprise. She hadn't actually spoken to Georgina properly, yet the whole time she had been living with her partner. It hit her how Georgina might be feeling about the situation and Emily felt terrible that she hadn't considered it before telling Rome she would live here with him instead of in Seth's cottage.

Emily hesitated for a second too long and it prompted Georgina to speak again.

"Did you get fired?" she said, candidly. Emily saw Rome look at Georgina. She cleared her throat.

"No, I quit actually," Emily replied, wishing they could talk about something else.

"Why was that? Did you prefer Rome's farm?" Georgina smiled but Emily couldn't help but feel like she was under interrogation and Georgina's intentions were not friendly ones.

"Emily doesn't have to tell us why she quit, Georgina," Rome said.

"No it's okay. I discovered my partner was cheating on me. My partner happened to be my boss." Emily was not proud as she said the words out loud.

"Oh I see. Sorry to hear that."

Emily highly doubted Georgina was sorry, judging by the smug look on her face. Rome and Seth looked uncomfortable but were silent as they finished off their dinner.

"The food was lovely, Emily thank you. I just don't have a big appetite tonight. I'm tired from traveling. I was up country competing my horses." Georgina gave a short smile and pushed her half-full plate forwards. Emily smiled politely and gathered the plates. Rome stood up and carried some things over to the sink. He stood close to Emily as he said under his breath.

"I'm sorry about her Emily. She's just jealous."

"No it's fine, really. She didn't do anything." Emily didn't want to cause drama. She knew how women could be. She didn't want Rome to be caught in a hard place because of friction between her and Georgina.

Emily bent to pull the apple crumble out of the oven. She took it out with a tea towel and placed it on the side. That was when she saw Rome's face fall. He stood there frozen as if he'd seen a ghost. He stared at the crumble. She looked at his face. His unblinking, glassy eyes.

"Rome, are you okay?" Emily asked quietly. "Do you not like apple crumble?"

Rome cleared his throat and flicked his gaze away.

"No it's nothing. I'm fine. I'm just going to run to the loo." He turned and left the kitchen quickly.

That was strange. She had clearly upset Georgina somehow and now Rome seemed annoyed as well. Rome returned a few minutes later as Emily scooped the crumble into four bowls and took them to the table with a pot of cream.

"I hope it's okay, everyone. I've never made it before." Emily saw Rome physically swallow and his face looked drawn and pale. She saw Georgina look at him and put a hand on his arm.

"Darling, you don't have to eat that," she said, flicking a scornful expression in Emily's direction.

"Georgina, it's fine," Rome said, in a hushed voice.

"I'm sorry. Have I done something to upset anyone?" Emily said. Even Seth looked grim.

"Have you not told her?" Georgina said, quietly. She looked up at Emily, hand still firmly on Rome's arm.

"Told me what?" Emily was confused now. She seemed to have managed to upset everyone with an apple crumble.

"It's not really any of your business anyway," Georgina said.

"Georgina don't start," Rome warned her. "It's fine, Emily. Nothing's wrong. This looks great, thank you." Rome picked up a spoon and started to eat. Seth followed suit and Georgina stabbed her spoon into the crumble, taking tiny bites. Emily watched them all carefully through the deafening silence as they ate. Rome was withdrawn. Seth, usually the more jolly and talkative one, was strangely quiet and sombre. Georgina seemed angry but from what Emily had seen of the woman so far it didn't seem too out of character. What had she done? Everyone finished and Rome placed his hand on Georgina's back.

"Shall I walk you out?" Rome stood up.

"So soon?" said Georgina.

"I'm tired and I suspect I'll be up and down in the night with the sheep. I need to get my head down for a bit," said Rome, as Georgina stood up and he led her to the door.

"Thanks for dinner, Emily," Georgina said, with her back to Emily as they left the kitchen. Emily heard the door shut and took a deep breath, then let it out in a silent sigh.

"I'd better get going too," said Seth, who was standing up and grabbing his crutches. "Dinner was amazing. Thank you."

Emily gave him a weak smile and he left.

Rome

"That was insensitive of her," said Georgina, as she turned to face Rome once the back door was shut.

"You know I haven't told her. She didn't do anything wrong. You were so rude in there," said Rome. "Just go home, Georgina. We'll talk about this tomorrow; I'm knackered." Rome crossed his arms over his body against the chilly night air.

"I want her out," said Georgina.

Rome took a deep breath and kept calm.

"I'm not talking about this right now, Georgina. Even if I asked Seth to move in with me and she lived in the cottage you'd still have a problem with her."

Rome walked towards the back door.

"We'll discuss this tomorrow Rome," she called after him.

He shut the door hard and walked back to the kitchen, where Emily was washing up.

"I can do that," he offered.

"It's okay. I'm almost done." Emily didn't look up at him as he spoke, keeping her eyes firmly on the sink.

"I'm sorry about Georgina. She was out of order. Just ignore her," he said, as he walked over and grabbed a tea towel. Rome started to dry the dishes as Emily washed.

"No, you don't have to apologise. I understand how Georgina must be feeling with another woman moving in. If it's going to cause trouble I can go."

There was no way Rome would let that happen.

"No, don't be silly. Of course you're staying. She'll get over it."

Emily smiled weakly as she finished washing the last plate and passed it to Rome to dry.

"I think I'm just going to go to bed," she said, and with a quick glance over at him, she turned and left the kitchen. Rome watched her bend to stroke the lamb on the head and then she was gone.

Rome put the plate down and gripped the counter top. He was finally alone, he didn't have to hold it in anymore. He let out a long, shaky breath. All he could think of right now was *her* and the long ago memories. He forced Georgina and Emily to the back of his mind as *she* took over. He felt her touch on his skin, her voice in his ear as goose bumps crawled up his body. He rifled through the top kitchen cupboard right at the back and pulled down a bottle. He unscrewed the top and swigged some back, trying to wash down the lump in his throat. She whispered to him, pulling him into the sorrowful dark. He took gulp after gulp until his throat burned. Heat filled his chest like a fire made worse by the effort not to let the tears out. His hand moved to his chest and he tilted his head back with his eyes closed and just stood there. His mind whirled, but he could feel the veil of alcohol begin to shroud him. It numbed the anxious, pressing memories, bringing a fog down over them so they were there but faded and more bearable. He drank until he felt detached, until his pain wasn't his own, until he was just someone else looking in.

Emily

Emily went to bed that night questioning everything: her place on the farm; Georgina and Rome; whether she had really done the right thing giving up on her old, comfortable, familiar life and plunging into this new utterly confusing one. Somehow she had upset Rome tonight but she had no idea how, which proved how much she didn't know about him. How long had she known him? Nearly a week? She loved the farm, there was no doubt about it, and she had learned so much. In some strange way she felt like this was the life she had been missing so she couldn't work out why everything was so confusing right now. Emily didn't want to question her decision, but she felt herself doing just that.

Her thoughts were disturbed by a loud thud, followed by the sound of shattering glass downstairs. Emily sat bolt upright in bed and clicked her phone beside her to see that it was past midnight. How long had she been awake, thinking? She turned back the bed cover and slipped on her white cotton dressing gown. Emily opened the door and tiptoed downstairs, praying it wasn't a burglar. Should she have brought a weapon? She peeked round the door silently and looked around the kitchen. Sprawled out on the floor by the sink was Rome. On the other side of the room were a startled dog and lamb. Tess was over by Rome, sniffing him gingerly.

Emily's stomach flipped as she rushed over, tightening the string on her dressing gown before bending down by his head. There was shattered glass around him. He had obviously knocked a glass down when he fell. The smell of alcohol filled her nostrils. She realised the smashed glass was a whisky bottle. Turning her attention to Rome, she shook him with a hand firmly on his shoulder.

"Rome, can you hear me?" she said, her heart rate doubled. He groaned quietly. "Can you get up, Rome? I think you need to get to bed."

He was silent. She noticed he was fully dressed still. He hadn't even slept tonight yet. Was this her fault? Had she upset him this much with that stupid apple crumble? Georgina had told him he didn't have to eat it if he didn't want to, like he was a child. Georgina had blamed Emily for something but she wasn't sure what it was yet. Emily didn't know what she was missing here. Now Rome had drunk himself into oblivion. She shook him again. She was worried that he had hurt his head when he fell. Should she call an ambulance? There was no signal. Did he have a landline? She couldn't leave him to run around desperately with her mobile searching for the farm's elusive signal.

"Rome." She shook him harder this time, becoming more and more agitated. She pulled his arms, which were heavy and floppy. She wracked her brains. Was he out from the alcohol or the fall? Losing patience from worry she stood up and went to the sink. Hastily, Emily filled a glass and then poured it straight down onto Rome's head. He stirred and spluttered. His eyes flicked open for a second and then closed again as he shuddered. She refilled the glass and splashed more water over his head. This time he opened his eyes and drew his hands closer into his body, pushing himself up a little as he coughed. He mumbled something but she couldn't make it out as she bent and grabbed his shoulders.

"Get up, Rome. Let's go upstairs," she said, loudly and clearly. He mumbled something again and went to lay his head back on the floor.

"No," she said. "Up." She knelt down on the floor, carefully avoiding the smashed glass. She gathered up the big chunks and moved them up onto the sideboard. There were only small shards left, which she would have to sweep up later. Emily grabbed his arms and pulled hard until she managed to get him into a sitting position. His head rolled forwards, onto her shoulder. His face pressed into her chest. She reached her arms under his and circled them around his back. Emily chewed on her lip, beginning to feel nervous that she wouldn't be able to get him off the ground.

"Rome, come on. Up you get." He groaned again. Awkwardly, she managed to get to her feet while still bending over, arms around him. It was like holding a stroppy toddler when they decided they didn't want to walk down the supermarket isle. Rome, however, probably weighed about one hundred and ninety pounds. His back was solid with muscle. She could barely get a good grip around him.

"Come on Rome. You'll have to help me. Up you get," she repeated, loudly. He stirred. She heaved as hard as she could, trying to lift with her legs, not her back. She got him off the floor and caught him up against her as he tipped forwards onto her for balance, wedging her between him and the kitchen counter. Her arms were looped around him. His were dangling by his sides, his head was on top of her shoulder and she felt his breath in her ear. Rome grew heavier as he relaxed onto her and Emily decided that there was no way she'd get him upstairs.

"Come on Rome. To the sofa. It's only fifteen feet away."

She shuffled around so that her back was in the direction of the sofa and he was against the sideboard. Ensuring she had a good grip she moved backwards, inching towards the sofa. He barely moved his legs. She held most of his weight as they crawled slowly backwards. He stumbled and knocked her back and she just managed to hold him up. It felt like an eternity before they reached the sofa. She turned him awkwardly and dropped him onto the cushions.

He slumped down and grunted. Emily lifted his legs on and manoeuvred his head so he was straight. She straightened and breathed heavily as she caught her breath and wondered what had driven him to put himself in this state. She wondered, but doubted, if this was the first time he had done this as she looked down at him. Should she leave him like this? What if he were sick? She bent and hauled him towards her, turning him sideways. The side of his face squished into the sofa and he snored. Emily was satisfied that if he were sick it would go on the floor. She got some cushions off the armchair and wedged them behind his back to steady him. Emily wiped some water off his face with the sleeve of her dressing gown. She patted it over his cheek bone, down his jawline.

Emily petted the dogs and told them to lie down. She carried the lamb back over to the rug and put it by the dogs. She stoked the fire and put two big logs on. That should last till the morning. Rome shuddered and Emily decided she should get him a blanket.

Emily stood outside Rome's bedroom door. She'd not been in there before. After a second's hesitation she pushed the door open and stepped into the dark room, flicking on the light. The room was similar to hers. The bed sheets and curtains were the same: white with little forget-me-not flowers. There was a chest of drawers. Two windows stood on opposite sides of the room, with a double bed in the middle and a dressing table next to it.

Emily pulled the duvet off the bed to take down to Rome. As she reached across to get a pillow something on the pine dressing table caught her eye. It was a picture, sitting in a frame. Putting the duvet down she walked around the bed to face the dressing table. She caught her reflection in the dusty mirror and grimaced at her knotty, ruffled, blond hair and tired face before looking down at the photo.

Carefully, Emily picked it up and held it before her. The frame contained a photograph of a couple on their wedding day. The woman was beautiful, with long blond hair curling down her back, tumbling to her waist. A flower garland sat on her head, while a gorgeous white dress hugged her delicate figure. She was tilted back by strong arms and locked in a kiss with the handsome man in a black suit. Emily could see their smiling mouths touching, and their eyes were creased with laughter. Although the photo was a little faded she could still make out the man's familiar face, with the messy but beautiful hair, the charming bone structure and jawline. Even if she hadn't been able to see his face, she would have known by the broad shoulders and towering height.

She had never seen Rome look as happy as he did in this photograph. The sun illuminated the couple against a backdrop of rows of trees. They were frozen in time in a glow of happiness. Rome was married? Or had been, but the woman clearly wasn't Georgina. They were divorced then. Emily turned the photo over, and found writing on the back. *Helen and Rome forever and always, 2015.* So her name was Helen. Emily could only assume they were married in 2015 and the picture had clearly been taken in the summer, judging by the trees in full bloom behind them and the sun shining down on them. It was almost May now. That meant the picture had been taken almost five and a half years ago.

Their marriage hadn't lasted long, yet they looked so happy in the picture it was hard to imagine anything breaking them up. Emily placed the frame down carefully. She looked at the other items on the dressing table. There were some ornaments but not many. She couldn't help herself and she slid the drawer open. It was empty. She shut it, feeling guilty for being so nosy and then rushed back to the duvet, bundled it up and carrying it downstairs along with a pillow.

Rome was exactly how she'd left him when she returned and the dogs and lamb were now fast asleep again in front of the fire. Emily draped the duvet over Rome. She lifted his head gently and tucked the pillow underneath. He stirred, his eyes flicking open and closed. He mumbled something.

"Helen?"

Emily's heart lurched. He'd said his wife's name. His eyes flickered.

"Helen, come back." His voice was raw and filled with pain. Emily watched as he began to cry, unsure whether to try and wake him or not. She shook him gently and knelt down beside him.

"Rome?" she said. His eyes opened and closed again.

"Helen, is that you?" he said, quietly. Suddenly his arms reached out and grabbed her. He pulled her closer. His hands were on her lower back as he pulled her in towards him. His eyes were open now as he held Emily against his chest. She lay there awkwardly against his hot, damp body. Maybe he didn't need the duvet.

"Helen, I knew it was you," he said. Emily put her hands against his body to push him away, gaining some space between them, fully aware that they were far too close.

"It's not Helen, Rome. It's Emily."

Rome seemed to see her now. "Emily?"

Emily pulled away from him. She felt his grip loosen from her back. He began to cry harder now.

"I thought she'd come back." His voice cracked.

Feeling confused and at a loss as to what to do Emily soothed him and smoothed his hair back. She stroked his face gently, rubbing her hand from his cheekbone back into his hair. He calmed down slightly and his eyes closed again. That was when Emily saw something glinting, lying against the fabric of his shirt on his chest. Two rings sat there on a thin chain.

She picked them up gently. They were wedding bands: a thin delicate one with small flowers engraved around it and a thicker, larger one designed for a man. Rome's wedding rings perhaps. One must have been Helen's. He was clearly upset about her. Emily wondered what had happened between them for Rome to still be clinging to her so tightly. She placed the rings back on his chest, which rose and fell gently. He was fast asleep now.

Emily spent ten more minutes cleaning up the broken glass and mopping up the water she'd used to wake him, then she went back to bed after one last glance at Rome.

*

The next morning, Emily got up at the crack of dawn. She dressed and gulped down a cup of tea in the kitchen while Rome continued to sleep. Emily strode out into the yard and put three round bales of silage in the hay rings for the cows, using the tractor. She managed to cut the plastic off the bales and do everything just as Rome had showed her. Farming wasn't so bad if you weren't afraid to get dirty. She checked the sheep and discovered one new lamb, which must have been born in the night. Rome obviously hadn't been out to check them. Emily felt guilty as she realised she should have thought about that and checked them herself but luckily the lamb and ewe seemed okay. She put them in one of the little hurdle pens and filled a bucket of water for the ewe, then grabbed an armful of hay and shoved it in the corner of the pen. One of the hay rings was running out so she got back in the tractor and put a bale in for them.

Emily fed Bramley the horse. She was still cautious of him and she threw some hay over his gate and gave him a pat on the neck, but she'd have to let Rome clean out his stable when he woke up later.

As Emily walked back up from the bottom of the farm towards the house, after completing the morning's jobs, she was met by a clatter of hooves in the yard. Georgina jumped down from a tall chestnut horse and tied it to a loop of baler twine on a rail of the garden fence. Emily saw her look over in her direction as she neared the house.

"Where's Rome?" she demanded. No greeting, but Emily guessed she had lost that right when she had ludicrously baked them all an apple crumble. Next time she'd be sticking to brownies.

"He's still asleep in the house," Emily replied. "I don't think he's feeling too well. I could get him to call you when he's up?"

"No, I'll go in and speak to him now," Georgina said, as she swung the gate open and marched towards the back door.

Emily watched her storm into the house. She always seemed angry about something.

Rome

Rome started awake and was alarmed to see Georgina's stern face glowering down at him. He pushed himself up a little and was going to speak but found his mouth was painfully dry. Rome touched a hand to his head as it throbbed and he tried to blink away his cloudy vision. His stomach churned.

"What are you still doing asleep? I just saw Emily out in the yard. Can she be trusted to feed the livestock on her own?" Georgina's voice hurt Rome's head and drilled through him. He sat up slowly and she moved back. He just needed some water. He wanted to drown his mouth in cool water. He rose to his feet and paused briefly to let the insistent throbbing in his skull subside a little before going to the sink to fill a glass. He gulped back the water and quenched his dry mouth.

"What's the time?" he said to Georgina, noticing how raspy his voice was.

"It's gone eight o'clock," she said. Rome looked at her face properly for the first time that morning. She was scowling, her eyes were wider than usual. Her lips were tightly closed together.

"What's wrong?" he asked. "Why are you here so early?"

"I went for an early morning hack from the manor, over the beach and then decided to come here to talk to you about last night. However, I can now see you've been drinking. I told you I wouldn't give you any more chances, Rome." She crossed her arms and stared at him. Rome moved his mouth to say something in his defence but had no idea what he could do now.

"Don't say anything. Don't try and lie. Don't try and get out of it, just face it. We're done." She turned to leave, and his stomach twisted into a ball of nerves. Now he was sure he'd be sick.

"Georgina, no!" he called after her. Panic gripped him. He quickly swiped back his hair and fastened an extra button on his shirt as he rushed to the door and forced his boots on. He stumbled out, flying after her. She was mounting her horse as he rushed down the garden path.

"Georgina. It was a relapse. Things got too much. You understand, don't you?" he pleaded.

She looked down on him from atop her horse.

"Yes, I understand, Rome. I've continued to relentlessly do so for a long time now. I'm done. Maybe this is what you need to snap you out of this habit of yours."

She clicked her horse and tapped him with her heels.

"Georgie, please. Let's talk," he called.

"We've had this talk for the last time, Rome." She urged on her horse and trotted down the farm track. Rome was dumbstruck. He shuddered but he barely noticed it as he watched her ride away. His safety, his last chance, rode away. He was finished. He turned, mouth gaping as he walked past Emily who he'd only just realised was stood by the garden gate. He walked down the garden path and into the house.

"Rome?" The voice woke him from his trance. It was Emily hovering in the doorway.

"Are you okay?" she asked, quietly. If Emily knew the severity of the situation, she wouldn't be asking that, that's why he held back a splutter of laughter. It wasn't her fault. She just didn't understand the dire consequences that Georgina leaving him would bring.

Rome turned to face her. His head throbbed, but the pain was nothing compared to the tight knot of fear in his stomach. He clenched his fists hard, wanting his knuckles to snap. He wanted to lose control but he didn't want to scare Emily, so, in that moment he kept a lid on it even though he didn't know how he managed to.

"It's complicated, Emily. More than meets the eye. You wouldn't understand." He heard his own voice quiver. He was aware of the fact that he probably looked like a mad man. The distance Emily was keeping between them was another clue. She hovered by the door, touching the frame, not willing to cross the threshold.

"The animals are done. There was a new lamb. They all look fine." She smiled faintly. The kind of smile people give you at a funeral. He didn't want her to pity him.

"That's great Emily, thank you. I just need to go and have a word with Seth." He ran a hand over his stubble, taking a deep breath. Would Seth be as devastated as he was?

"Do you want to talk about it?" Emily asked. She slipped her hand from the door frame and entered the room. She leant against the side board.

"You don't want to know." Rome moved towards the door. He passed Emily and went to open the back door.

"How do you know that?" she asked. Rome kept his cool. She wouldn't be hounding him if she knew how he was writhing inside.

"Emily, I really need some time alone," he snapped, slamming the door on his way out as his anger boiled over. With crimson clouded vision he headed straight for Seth's cottage. Seth would know what to do. He *had* to know, because Rome couldn't even contemplate the disaster that would unfold if he couldn't fix this.

Emily

It was a clear, warm morning and Emily was down in the lambing shed with the ewes. At least fifty must have lambed now. It was madness. She and Rome had barely slept. Emily felt like she hadn't left the lambing shed. She'd had no time to think about Mark or her old job. She had just thrown herself into this and hadn't got a moment of peace since it had started. It was the beginning of May and Rome said it would peak now and they'd have all of them lambed in the next two weeks. Seth went out each night and checked them, although he couldn't really intervene, but if he had a problem he came to fetch Rome. Emily hadn't showered since the day before yesterday. The novelty of showering after every sheep birth had worn off fast. As the new born lambs grew stronger they released them back into the main flock. This way, they had enough hurdle pens for the new lambs, which were being born more and more frequently.

Things had been tense since Rome's break up with Georgina. He hadn't spoken much, hadn't eaten much. She wasn't even confident he'd taken a shower. It had been three days now.

Emily left the lambing shed and was going to make her way back to the house for a tea break when the apple orchard slid into her thoughts. If she went left and past the bottom of the farmhouse garden she could go back through that little gate to the orchard and see it again. Emily hesitated, but her nosy side managed to get the better of her and then she couldn't get there fast enough.

Emily pushed on the gate and shoved her way into the overgrown fruit garden. The orchard was filled with pink apple blossom. She looked around, taking in the wild hedges, the out of control trees, the wispy, weedy grass. She tried to imagine what it might look like if someone gave it some love and time. That was when the thought came to her: she would do it. It was a big job but it wasn't like she was doing much at the moment when they weren't lambing. She didn't know a lot about apple trees but how hard could it be? She just needed to trim the hedges, mow the grass, prune the trees, burn the stuff she cut off. Easy.

An hour had passed and Emily didn't think she'd sweated so much in all of her life. She had found one of those push along mowers with the blades that span as you pushed it, with no engine. It was clearly not designed for grass like this. She pushed it and unblocked it and pushed it again. She had made it down one line of grass between the trees so far. There must have been about ten rows and she had done *one*. She stopped and wiped sweat from her brow. If she was going to do this she was going to have to buy a mower.

Rome

Over the last few days, Rome had spent most of his time coming up with a plan to get Georgina back. He had spoken in depth with Seth and he was confident he could get her back. He was going to see her tonight. He was going to drive over to the Addleton estate right after he'd showered. Emily would be able to cover things.

Emily had been a blessing. With everything going on in his head and Seth's leg, she had taken so much of the work load off. He couldn't believe how fast she had gotten the hang of everything. She had just fitted right in. He knew he would have to make it up to her when this was sorted. He knew he'd been snappy and harsh. If Emily knew what was on the line, though, she would understand why he was so upset. He couldn't tell her. No one could ever truly understand why he had to do this. He pushed it to the back of his mind. Whether it was right or not, Rome had to do this. It didn't matter if it was the last thing he wanted. He steeled himself ready for their meeting later on.

That evening Rome was in his Landrover, driving back from his meeting with Georgina. It had gone okay. She had been more understanding than he'd thought she would. Seth was right: she liked that he had come after her, that he had driven to the manor house to find her. He had apologised and promised her he wouldn't get into that state again. He knew what he had done was wrong: he had shown himself up in front of Emily by getting drunk, neglected his animals. They could have been hurt because of him.

He had squandered his last chance with Georgina, but there was hope. She had agreed to come and meet him tomorrow at the farm. He promised her he'd have something special planned. He was going to ask Emily to watch the sheep while he took Georgina on a picnic. He was going to take her to the top of the valley so they could take in the view over Addleton and the farmyard below. He had something he needed to ask her.

*

Rome parked his Landrover in the yard and headed indoors. The smell of food filled his nostrils as he walked through the door and his stomach rumbled instantly. Emily was in the kitchen cooking. She was wearing her short dressing gown, which grazed her thighs. Her hair was wrapped up in a towel.

"Hey," he greeted her as he walked in. "That smells good."

He sat down at the kitchen table and his dogs swarmed around his legs.

"Just making us a quick bolognaise. Another ewe lambed when you were gone but it went fine. She didn't need much help," Emily said, with her back to him as she stirred the pot.

"That's good, then. Thank you for all of your help Emily. I really couldn't have done this without you," Rome said. Emily smiled at him.

"Thank you for having me here. I've enjoyed it."

Rome would miss that smile if he had to send Emily away. He would miss *her*. He had taken her for granted the last few weeks. He liked her company. She was relaxed, easy going, funny and kind. He was hoping if all went well with Georgina tomorrow then Emily would be able to stay. He wasn't sure what he could do if Georgina insisted he make her leave.

He watched Emily reach up to get two plates from the top cupboard. He drew his eyes away from the backs of her thighs as her dressing gown rose a little. It was things like that he knew he should absolutely not be noticing. Emily brought him over a plateful of bolognaise, along with a knife and fork. Her sweet, alluring perfume caught his attention as she put the plate down.

"Thanks a lot," he said. He hadn't been eating properly with everything that was going on. He knew they were supposed to be taking turns with the cooking, but Emily just seemed to be doing it. He'd come in and she would already be cooking. Emily sat down opposite him and they ate in silence for a minute. He looked over at her and forced his eyes upwards before they lingered too long on the way her dressing gown opened at her chest.

"I just wanted to say sorry, Emily. I've not been myself the last few days. It's being sorted out though. I wanted to apologise for the other night as well when I lost my temper after my argument with Georgina. You probably think I'm terrible."

"Everyone has bad days," she said. Rome felt guilty about how understanding she was. She should be disgusted by his behaviour. He smiled at her, thinking for one short second that he might be able to trust Emily to share his problems with. But no, he couldn't tell her; she would think he was awful.

"How are you anyway? Has it been okay here or do you miss home?" he asked.

"It's nice to be away. I don't miss Mark. I barely saw him anyway. I don't miss the flat, not when I'm surrounded by the farm," Emily said, looking at him.

"That's good to hear. I'm happy you like it here," he said, earnestly.

*

Emily and Rome sat in the living room that night after checking the sheep. Emily was feeding the orphan lamb its bottle on the rug. He had gotten used to it being inside. He normally left them outside but it made Emily happy to have him in. Rome would say it was the city girl in her but Helen used to do it too. It took him back as he slouched on the sofa with his dogs' heads in his lap. If he squinted a little Helen could have been in the room with him. Emily was so similar to her: her hair, her temperament. Rome wondered if it was that which was drawing him to Emily. He relished the feeling. He knew he shouldn't trick himself but for a moment he imagined himself back in time, before Helen had gone. When they were happy. Rome couldn't imagine how *anyone* could be as happy as they were. It was only as Emily's voice broke the silence that he realised he'd let himself imagine too hard.

"Are you okay, Rome?" Emily had finished feeding the lamb. "You're crying."

Rome cleared his throat. He swiped at his face. How hadn't he noticed?

"I'm not, I'm fine," he said, unconvincingly.

"You're not fine. You were crying. What's the matter?" she asked as she held her hands out to the lamb, which was searching for more milk.

"It's nothing really." How could he explain it all to her? He felt his chest tighten. Rome wanted Emily to look away. He didn't let others see him cry. He didn't cry. He told himself he wouldn't now but he could feel the emotion building in his chest. His throat tightened and his eyes burned as he fought it. The only cure was the whisky, but he'd promised Georgina. He would at least be faithful to his promise.

"You can talk to me if you want, you know. I know we don't really know each other that well. I know it's only been two weeks but we've seen each other every day. It feels like longer to me. You can trust me." Emily was quiet as she looked at him. Rome stroked Birdie's head to calm his anxious hand. He couldn't fight it any longer and tears began to fall.

How could he do this in front of Emily? Emily stood up as he wiped his eyes. The emotion filled his whole body and his chest heaved as he let it out. The dogs lifted their heads and jumped down to Emily as she crossed the room. Emily offered her hand to Rome and he found himself taking it. He craved the bottle.

He wanted to numb this. He wanted to stop feeling it but the guilt of his promise bore down on him. Emily's hand fit inside his and she pulled him up off the sofa, straight into her arms. He found himself sinking into her. Her arms were round him, stroking up and down his back. His head was on her shoulder, his face in her silky hair. Their bodies were close as Emily comforted him. Rome clutched the soft fabric of Emily's pyjamas and he cried. No one had ever held him while he cried. No one except Helen. He breathed Emily in, soaking up the comfort as her hands soothed him. The pain in his chest was unbearable. He couldn't stop reliving that day in his head. The day that broke him.

"It's my wife," he choked out, as he gripped Emily for support. He wasn't sure how much longer he could stay standing. He pictured the bottle in the back of the cupboard. He felt his body crave it.

"What happened?" she said, softly. Rome felt sick as the brutal images of that day came flooding back.

"I lost her," he croaked. Emily didn't push him or force him to speak. She just held him until he was ready. Rome played the day over and over in his head. He replayed the moment in excruciating clarity.

"She died." His stomach turned violently every time he said those words. He cracked and from then he couldn't keep it in as his breathing became erratic. Years of pent up sorrow wracked his body and he choked and sobbed into Emily's shoulder. He didn't consider what she might think about him. He didn't care. He just let it flow out. He pictured Helen's face, the way it had looked after the accident. He forced in a breath and choked it back out. Emily held him tightly and didn't say a word.

Half an hour later they were sat on the sofa and Rome's shaking hand was holding a cup of coffee Emily had made for him. He breathed deep shuddering breaths but he had run out of tears. Emily had held Rome until he had stopped crying and then she had sat him down on the sofa and placed a cup of coffee into his hand. Some had spilt as he shook but she had cleaned it up. Emily was opposite him now with a cup of tea in one hand and the other placed gently on his knee as he calmed down.

"You don't have to tell me about it, Rome. Not if you're not ready," she assured him. He sipped his coffee. He wanted to get it out. He was ready to tell her. Rome took a moment to compose himself before he began.

"We had been married for two years. We had celebrated our anniversary a couple of weeks before she died. This summer will be three years since that day. She'd only gone out to the village. There was an accident: a driver passing through. He was drunk." Rome took in a shuddering gulp of air.

"He smashed into Helen's truck and she was rushed to hospital. I didn't know straight away because of the signal here. No one could reach me on my phone, but one of the guys from the village who knew me and Helen drove up to get me. He'd seen the accident. I remember the feeling when he told me there'd been an accident. I still feel it every day: the anxiety and the sheer panic. The numbness in my brain. The disbelief mixed with the fear." Rome took a break and wiped his eyes on the back of his hands. Emily gently squeezed his knee for reassurance.

"I don't remember the drive to the hospital. The guy, Sammy, he drove me. I ran in, I went up to the desk and said her name. They showed me through to a doctor. He stood in front of me and told me they had done everything they could but …" He wavered as he looked at Emily and tried to press on with the agonising story. "But she hadn't pulled through." His voice quivered and he halted again. Emily gave him a faint, reassuring smile. He went on with a shake in his voice, "My world just ended. I couldn't believe it at first, I asked to see her and they led me through. She was bruised, covered in blood, still … cold. She was gone."

He paused again.

"I wanted to die. The thought of living without her was too much. I collapsed and I didn't stand again until two nurses dragged me up off the floor. I lay next to her on the bed and I just held her for as long as I was allowed. When I got home I had to tell Seth. Seth was Helen's brother. *Is* Helen's brother. My brother-in-law. He was distraught. The days that followed were the hardest of our lives. I don't know how I kept going. I don't know why I did but I knew Helen would have wanted me to."

"It was only a few days after that I actually thought about the man that had done it. I wanted to kill him." Rome shook his head with a clenched jaw and started to cry silently before he could say any more. Saying it all out loud was always hard. Once again, Emily held him. She took his mug, put it down and held Rome's head against her chest.

"I just don't know how to be without her," he whispered.

Emily

Emily helped Rome to bed. They walked upstairs together and she followed him to his bedroom. He pulled his shirt off over his head, dropped his jeans, barely aware that Emily was there as he climbed into bed.

"Do you need anything?" she asked him. He shook his head. "Well, you know where I am."

She turned to leave.

"Actually, Emily." He paused for a second. "No, forget it."

"Go on," she said.

"You don't have to. But I was wondering if you'd lie here with me for a bit. Just talk to me so I stop thinking about it."

"Of course I will." She walked over to lie on top of the duvet but Rome had already lifted it for her to get under. She couldn't help but think of Georgina as she slid in next to Rome. They lay there facing the ceiling in the dark and they chatted about sheep and cows. They talked about everything they'd done on the farm the last few weeks and Emily talked about the first time she'd lambed a ewe with Seth. Rome talked for a while but then he was quiet and just listened to Emily as she talked about her old life and Mark and her parents. Soon she was feeling tired and they just lay there in silence.

Emily woke up the next morning and was immediately aware of the feeling of someone pressing against her. For a split second she thought she was back at home with Mark but, as her mind cleared, she saw she was in Rome's bedroom. She slowly slipped out from under the covers and got up from the bed. Rome's bare chest was exposed and his head was tilted back. His and Helen's rings rested against his skin. His eyes were shut and he looked peaceful.

It had hurt Emily, listening to him the night before. She had cried silently while he had sobbed on her shoulder. She'd never seen someone in so much pain before. There was nothing she could do to make it better and she had felt helpless. She thought about the blond woman's sweet face in the photo she had seen on the dressing table. Rome's wife. Their future had been stolen away by a careless driver. Emily thought back to her own terrifying car accident; the way the driver had come out of nowhere and caved into the side of her car. She had survived, though, she had been luckier than Helen.

Emily tiptoed from the room, back to hers. She didn't want Rome to think she'd stuck around. She hadn't meant to fall asleep there.

Rome

Rome opened his eyes as he heard Emily leave the room. He shouldn't have asked her to sit with him. They'd ended up falling asleep together. He flung back the covers, pissed off with himself. He put on the clothes that were heaped on the floor and jogged downstairs. Tension gripped him as he remembered that today was the day. He had to deal with the animals and meet Georgina. They were going to meet in the farmyard at eight so they could have an early morning walk. He flicked on the kettle and ran his hand through his hair. His eyes hurt, feeling swollen and dry. He made a coffee and drank it down, then headed out the back door.

By eight o'clock Rome had finished the jobs. He had seen Seth in the lambing pen, where four lambs had been born in the night. Seth said it had all gone fine and he had managed even though Rome told him he should have asked for help. Rome normally woke around one and he'd go out and check on them but he'd slept soundly last night. He would have to start setting alarms. He couldn't let Seth do all the work. Rome headed across the yard where Georgina was waiting for him outside the garden gate. He smiled at her and walked over. They kissed briefly.

"I'll go in and get the stuff quickly," he said, and headed indoors. He was back a few minutes later with a carrier bag full of sandwiches and coffee. It wasn't very romantic but it was the best he could manage.

"Your eyes look red," Georgina said. She looked at him as they walked across the yard towards the field.

"Yeah I got some spray in them this morning when I was treating a sheep's foot. I washed it out though, they're fine now," he lied. It was for the best.

She seemed to accept it as they went through the wooden gate and began climbing the gentle slope to the top of the valley. The early morning sun was rising. The air was fresh and warm with the promise of summer. Rome's body was cold. His palms sweated. He felt as though there was lead in his boots as they walked up the field. Every step became heavier than the one before. They reached the top and sat on the grass.

He looked out across the landscape, at his and Seth's farm, the village a few miles below across the valley and the marshes beyond. He could see the lambing shed in the distance. He could see Seth's cottage and behind he saw the pink blossom of Helen's orchard. She used to spend hours in there admiring the blossom. She would sit out there with Birdie and Tess and drink tea in a world of her own. He could picture the wooden swing hanging under the weeping willow. Rome saw her now as clear as day in his mind's eye as she laughed and swung back and forth then jumped off and ran into his arms. Goosebumps spread over his body as he imagined what once was but would never be again. Rome had scattered Helen's ashes in the orchard and from that day he had never set foot in there again. His heart couldn't take the memories.

Georgina spoke then, shattering the memories.

"So, shall we talk about it?"

"What is it exactly that you want to talk about?" Rome asked, trying to keep his voice even.

"The fact that you drank the other night after I gave you one last chance not to screw up," she said. Rome took a deep breath.

"I promised you I wouldn't drink again Georgina and so far I've kept that promise," he said. He wasn't sure why he'd brought food with them. He felt too sick to eat.

"What happens if you break it?" she said.

"I won't. I know I made a mistake. I'm not going to let myself get into that state again. I regret it," he said. It was partly true. Georgina smiled at him.

"I love you Rome. I'm doing this for your own good." She touched his arm. Rome forced a smile.

"I love you too." He thought of Helen as he said it. It was one of the hardest things for him to say those three words to Georgina. He had only loved one woman. He was certain he wouldn't love again but he would tell Georgina what she wanted to hear. It was time. He felt the weight of it in his pocket. He felt his stomach churn and he swallowed down the lump in his throat as he forced his eyes onto Georgina. He told himself it meant nothing. He was doing it for Helen. It was for the best. Rome took a deep breath and quickly grabbed Georgina's hand before he could change his mind.

"I have something to ask you," he said. Georgina faced him with an eager expression. Did she know what he was about to do? Rome took it from his pocket. He held out the ring and tried to keep it together. He thought of Helen's face. Georgina's mouth made an 'o' shape and she put a hand on her chest. Rome held her hand a little tighter, only to try and mask the shake in his own.

"I know it's not the best timing but it took losing you to make me realise I never want to be without you. Will you marry me?"

He choked out the words in one breath before he could change his mind. Never had he uttered a sentence more untrue. He pictured the day he had proposed to Helen in the orchard. He remembered it with such clarity: the exact way the sun was shining down on them as if they were the only two in the world, the way the hedge birds had sung just for them, Helen's face as she burst into tears and threw her arms around his neck, the touch of her lips as they kissed while he slipped the ring onto her finger.

"Rome. I mean, it's a lot. We almost just broke up … but," she paused for a second. "But yes. I'll marry you. I love you." She held her finger out so Rome could put the ring on. This was so far from his proposal to Helen it was almost laughable.

Emily

Emily had just finished mowing part of the orchard. She had gone into the village and bought a mower from the hardware shop and two cans of fuel from the fuel station. She had walked all the way down the farm track to get her car from the end. She had then had to lug the mower all the way down the rutted track. It had taken her a while to figure out how to work it, since she hadn't used a mower before. Once she managed to get it to work she had battled the orchard for about two hours on a high setting. She left the grass fairly long but she figured she could clip it shorter on the next run round and then it wouldn't be so difficult to push the mower through. She finished about half. The other half would have to wait until tomorrow. She was exhausted.

Emily made her way back to the farmyard. Just before she rounded the corner to lead her to the farmhouse front door, she heard a stranger's voice and then Rome's reply. Emily stopped and listened.

"You'd better be serious. If I find out this is so you can make your debt disappear you can have full faith that I will make you seriously regret it," a rough, male voice said.

"I love her," Rome's voice replied. Something flipped in Emily's stomach. Who did he love? He must be talking about Georgina.

"If I find out you're playing a game I'll–"

"You'll what?" Rome interjected. "Kill me? Yeah I got it. I'm busy, I have a lot to do. Goodbye."

Emily heard the scuff of his boots walking away.

"Marriage is a big commitment. You've already done it once. If you're not sure then don't lead her on," the man's voice said. Rome's boots stopped. Emily's heart beat faster. Was he going to marry Georgina?

"I'm sure. I proposed. I wouldn't have done it if I weren't sure. It's not about the money. I'm just ready to move on and start again with someone new."

So he had proposed. Emily's heart sank. She didn't want to hear any more. She turned quietly and headed back down towards the orchard. It was only last night he had sobbed into her shoulder about his wife and now he was saying to this man he was ready to marry somebody else. Why were they talking about Rome owing money?

Something in Emily burned to learn the truth and see clearly. She hadn't realised Rome was considering remarrying. But then, she hadn't know him long. She thought she knew him but she clearly didn't have his character pinned down. She hadn't realised she had felt a connection to Rome until she had heard this news, and realised how utterly disappointed she now felt.

Rome was keeping secrets, that was for sure. Something niggled at Emily to find out what they were.

*

Emily mulled over it all in the orchard for half an hour, pacing. She was in two minds. Firstly this was not her business, this had nothing to do with her and she should definitely not be upset about Rome's proposal. On the other hand she wanted answers. She wanted to know why the other man had accused Rome of proposing just to clear his debt. Who did he owe? She was also realising whatever she had been sensing between her and Rome was simply friendliness and nothing more. He loved somebody else. It wasn't like she could be upset. She had only realised a hint of what she might have wanted when it was gone. She was too late now. Emily thought back to Rome's reaction the day he had woken with a hangover and Georgina had confronted him and broken things off. Rome had told Emily she didn't understand what was going on and that it was complicated. What was complicated?

Emily left the orchard and walked down the path towards Seth's cottage. She glanced behind her and then knocked on the door before she changed her mind. Seth answered.

"Hi Emily, how are you?" he asked, with a smile.

"Actually, I was wondering if I could have a chat. Inside maybe," she said.

Seth stepped aside on his crutches, his smile fading at Emily's seriousness. "Come in."

The cottage was open plan, with the kitchen and lounge in the same room. It looked cosy.

"Everything okay?" said Seth. "Have a seat."

He gestured towards the sofa and Emily sat. The cottage had big windows and sunlight streamed through, setting the lounge in a warm glow.

"Can I get you a drink?" he asked.

"No, I'm fine. I actually wanted to talk about Rome."

Seth took a seat in an armchair opposite her. "Okay. What's it about?" he asked.

"I know it's none of my business but I'm quite confused to be honest. I just caught the tail end of a conversation between Rome and another man. I'm worried about him," said Emily. Seth shifted in his seat.

"What's worried you?" he asked.

"I know about Helen. I know that Rome is your brother-in-law and you lost your sister," Emily continued. "I'm sorry to hear that by the way. Rome was in a bad way the other night. He'd had a lot to drink and then he got very upset. He was inconsolable, actually. He is clearly still grieving badly for Helen."

Emily rubbed her hands nervously up and down her thighs.

Seth looked grave for a moment, his eyes downcast. "It was a horrible tragedy, the worst thing to get over for both of us. He's getting there, though. It's sweet of you to be concerned."

"No, it's not just that. It was what I just heard in that conversation. I think Rome has proposed to Georgina."

"Okay. And that worries you, why?"

"He's clearly not over Helen. He's in a lot of pain and is obviously using drink to ease that. Do you really think he is in the right frame of mind to remarry?" Emily said. Seth took a few seconds and then looked up at her.

"We can't know what's in Rome's head. If he's ready then he's ready," he said.

Emily didn't say anything for a while and she considered how far was too far. She knew she was sticking her nose in.

"I know it's not my place. This has nothing to do with me but this just feels like the wrong decision. It doesn't make sense," she said. "Maybe you could talk to him?" she continued before Seth could reply. "There's also something else I'm wondering about."

"What?" Seth asked.

"The man who Rome was speaking to mentioned a debt. He seemed to suggest Rome might be wanting to marry Georgina to clear this debt. Honestly, I can't help but wonder if he's right. I saw the pain Rome was in the other night. He is hurting. Someone can't be in that much pain one day and be ready to marry a few days later. And they had just broken up," Emily said. She felt like she was crossing a line but she didn't want to see Rome get hurt. Seth was silent for a while.

"Emily, I'm sure he knows what he's doing. And as far as the debt goes, yes, we do owe a bit of money but it's not something he would want to talk about."

"I think someone needs to talk to him," said Emily. "I don't think he's thinking clearly. I think grief is making him act out. How could he marry someone just to clear a debt? There must be another way to pay." She stood up. All she could think about was talking to Rome and trying to help him see sense, not for her benefit but for his.

"Emily wait." Seth started. "It's a little more confusing than you know."

"So enlighten me," she said, sitting back down.

"You're a very determined woman."

"I'll take that as a compliment," she crossed one leg over the other.

"Rome does owe money. We both do. We owe rent to our landlord," Seth said.

"You don't own the farm?"

"No. Helen and I were raised here by our parents. Helen loved it more than any of us. We lost our mother when we were children, and we lost our father shortly after Rome arrived here. Rome moved over from Ireland years ago for work. He and Helen met and fell in love very fast. He ended up moving in and helping us out. He also pumped all of his savings into the farm so we could afford the rent. We managed to pay it thanks to him. It was tough but we did it. Helen's business brought a lot in. She had an orchard. It's just a little way down the path from here."

Emily resisted to urge to clasp a hand to her mouth. She had been mowing Helen's orchard. She wondered if she had overstepped a line. Had she intruded? Seth continued.

"She grew apples and made cider. It was very profitable. We had our own brewery down behind the farmhouse. When Helen died Rome didn't want to carry it on. Firstly, we didn't know a lot about how to run it; it was Helen's thing. And secondly we just found it too painful. So, we struggled more with the rent. We ended up with a backlog and we're fighting to pay it off. If we don't, then we'll lose the farm and, honestly, I think it will destroy Rome. Don't get me wrong, I will be devastated. I was raised here. I've lost my family and I'm the last one left. The farm is the only thing I have. Rome feels the same. He will do anything to keep it, to keep Helen's legacy alive." Seth sounded hurt. Emily saw his eyes were glassy as he finished talking. She felt a surge of pain for Seth. She had no idea he had lost his entire family.

"So what are you saying?" she asked. "Rome is marrying for money, isn't he?"

"This won't sound great, Emily. Our landlord, Andrew Dawson, is a horrible, horrible man. Nasty peace of work. He is Georgina's father. Rome is insistent that he wants to marry her. He knows it will save the farm."

Emily's gut twisted. So he was doing this for the farm, not for love.

"So he doesn't love her?" she asked.

"No. He doesn't particularly like her at all. She's a cruel woman to be honest, not unlike her father in that respect. She hides it well enough but I know the real her. But this is why you can't say anything Emily. He knows what he's doing. He can't cope with losing the farm so he's doing the only thing possible to save it."

Emily sat silently as she absorbed the information. She had no idea how confusing everything was. Under the calm, beautiful surface of Bramblewood Farm there was pain and suffering. Emily felt sad for Rome, but also a little angry. She couldn't help but feel for Georgina at the same time. Even after the way Georgina had been towards her this wasn't exactly fair. She obviously thought Rome loved her. He didn't just not love her, he actively disliked her, by the sounds of things.

"He can't do this," said Emily.

"Emily please," Seth said. "You can't say anything. At the end of the day, it's not our business who he marries. He made this choice. No matter what you do, I promise you won't change his mind. He will do anything to keep this farm, no matter who he hurts in the process, including himself."

Emily left Seth's cottage, half wishing she had never stuck her nose in. How could she sit on this information? How could she be okay with the fact that Rome was grieving for his dead wife and marrying a woman he didn't love just so he could keep the farm Helen grew up on? Emily couldn't work out if he was sweet, cruel or delusional. Maybe he was all three, but she did know that since her conversation with Seth, she had lost a little respect for Rome. How could he do this to himself and to Georgina?

Rome

Andrew had finally left. Rome knew he'd have something to say about his proposal to his daughter, but that couldn't be helped. Rome was in the kitchen, his dogs were by his side as his forehead rested on the table. He didn't stir even when the back door opened.

"Rome?" It was Emily.

He sighed deeply and raised his head from the table.

"Is everything all right?" he said.

Emily took a seat opposite him and the lamb in the living room bleated and ran over. It bunted her leg searching for milk and she held her hand out to it.

"What's up?" she asked him.

Everything, he thought.

"Nothing," he said.

He gazed into the empty space of the living room. He didn't feel like talking to Emily, to anyone. The only company he thought he might welcome was a whisky bottle. He shifted his eyes to Emily. She tucked a strand of blond hair behind her ear. She had a strange expression on her face, one he hadn't seen before.

"What's up with you?" he said. He knew he sounded grumpy but his best efforts couldn't mask it. She opened her mouth and closed it again. She looked at him.

"I know you proposed to Georgina," she said. Great, she wanted to talk about the one thing he was desperately trying to let his mind escape from.

"And?"

"I know it's none of my business. I know I haven't been here that long. I'm sure you have a good reason but–" she paused.

"Go on," he said, praying this conversation could be over so he could let his mind go elsewhere.

"I accidently caught the end of your conversation with Andrew Dawson," she said. His stomach flipped.

"How do you know his name?" he said, looking at her now. She looked at him too, with a worried, awkward expression, on her face.

"I know it's none of my business, but I can't help what I heard. I went to speak to Seth. I was worried about you. I know why you're proposing and I don't think you should do it," she said, speaking quickly.

Rome was silent. He felt anger growing inside him. The last thing he needed was more people knowing his secret. He was angry with Seth for talking about their private business. He was angry with Emily for bringing it up. He was angry that she would think badly of him now. Most of all, he was furious that his plan was at risk now Emily knew the truth.

"No, it's *not* your business." He took a deep breath and looked down at the table as he rubbed his hands up and down his thighs. He bit down on his bottom lip. He didn't look at her as he spoke.

"It's more complicated than you know. This is something I have to do and unless you have three million pounds knocking around to buy this place then this is how it's going to be," he said, forcefully.

There was silence for a moment before Emily spoke.

"And what about Georgina?" Emily demanded. "She loves you doesn't she? Don't you think she deserves someone who loves her too?"

Rome was a little taken aback. He hadn't expected Emily to speak so candidly.

"You know nothing about Georgina. I can't talk about this." He didn't look at her as he rose from his chair. The legs scrapped against the wooden floor. He made for the back door and whistled for his dogs. He just needed to be alone.

Emily

The curtains in Emily's bedroom fluttered softly in the cool night breeze. No matter what she did, Emily couldn't sleep. She turned over in bed with a huff as she reached out to check the time on her phone. One o'clock. She'd been in and out of sleep all night. Her mind was too active to rest. Whatever she did, she couldn't help but think about Rome and the terrible decision he was making. She couldn't get involved though. It wasn't her place. She had already crossed the line by bringing it up with him and she had driven a wedge between them when things had been going well. She thought about Mark that night as well. He hadn't called her. He obviously didn't give a damn. Her side of the bed had probably already been filled. She still had to get the rest of her stuff back.

Emily flung back the covers. She felt flustered and hot. She took a shirt off the floor and buttoned it on then pulled on jeans and tied her hair up. Emily left her bedroom quietly so she didn't wake Rome and she tiptoed downstairs. She snuck past the lamb and dogs in the living room. Birdie lifted her head but didn't get up.

"Good girl," Emily whispered as she drifted through the living room. She picked up her coat, which was on the back of the chair at the kitchen table, and she slipped it on.

As she opened the back door, and quietly closed it behind her, she took in a deep breath of the cool night air. It was so fresh out there. It was like the air had a different taste than in the city. It was as satisfying as going for an hour's run and gulping fresh water at the end, refreshing and calming.

Emily wandered across the yard by the light of moon. The moon was full tonight casting a ghostly light over the farm. The cows were lying down in the shed as she walked through the night shadows on her way to the lambing shed. The troublesome thoughts in her mind subsided as she made her way through the silent farmyard until she came to the shed. Movement caught her attention at the back of the barn. Rome was already in there. He hadn't seen her yet. Maybe she should slip away but, as she went to go, his head whipped round.

"Emily?"

He must have heard her.

"Yes," she answered.

"Quick, get in here." She could hear the urgency in his voice. Adrenaline took over and she ran to the gate and over to where Rome was crouched amid the straw. A wet lamb lay limp at his boots. He was rubbing its belly.

"You need to revive this one. I've got another over here and the lamb is stuck and she's not doing well," he said, as he rushed away over to another ewe, which was panting on the ground. Emily panicked for a second. She knew the theory behind it but, when it came down to doing it, it still wasn't second nature to her. It was still stressful. She bent by the lamb and scrabbled for a blade of straw. She poked it up each nostril to clear the nasal passage in an attempt to get a response.

"You're fine. Do it just like you did it the first time with Seth," Rome called over. The words did little to comfort Emily but thinking of the first time she had lambed a ewe made her feel more confident now. She rubbed the lamb's belly up and down fast. The mother sheep was lying in front, making deep bleating noises for its baby. Emily stood up and lifted the limp lamb. She held it by its back legs and swung it from side to side. She held the legs in one hand and rubbed it up and down with the other. She swung again and then laid it back in the straw. She rubbed again and tried the straw a second time. Nothing was happening.

"It's not working," she called to Rome, panic rising inside her. He was behind a sheep, heaving the back legs of a lamb.

"Don't worry about it. If it's dead, it's dead," he called back.

"What, just give up?" Anger prickled in her chest.

"You can't save them all," he grunted, as he heaved the lamb from the sheep. It bobbed its wobbly head as Rome cleared the mucus from its nose and mouth. He placed it by the mother making bleating noises. She licked her lamb. Emily continued rubbing her lamb. Rome came over covered with afterbirth. His clothes were wet and the moonlight highlighted the glistening sweat trickling down his nose. He stood over Emily and the lamb.

"Do something," she said, looking up at him. Why wasn't he doing anything?

"Emily, sometimes you have to let nature take its course. This one didn't make it," he said, calmly.

"Aren't you upset?" she asked, concerned at how little he seemed to care about the lamb. "Don't you care that it died?"

"Of course I care. You just can't expect them all to come out healthy. You get used to it after years of doing it," he said. Emily stood up and looked down at the wet lamb. It was still. She felt tears brimming in her eyes and she wiped them away with her shirt sleeve before they fell.

"It gets easier. It's just farming," he said, touching her gently on the arm. Emily didn't reply. She heard the mother sheep bleat again. She wanted her lamb. Rome leant down and picked up the lamb by its back legs and carried it towards the gate.

"Where are you taking it?"

"I can't leave it in there. I'll have to get it collected tomorrow," he said. Emily followed him out the gate and closed it behind her. She watched the lamb dangling from his hand.

"Don't carry it like that," she said, jogging up behind him.

"It's dead."

Emily stopped.

"Why are you being so cold?" she said.

He stopped and turned. "I know it looks harsh, Emily, but this is what it is to be a farmer. Not all babies make it when they're born in hospitals, do they? Animals are no different."

"But you don't care," she said. She saw him look at her, his expression pained.

"I do care. I care a lot, but I can't cry over every dead one, Emily," he said. His voice softened slightly. "I remember my first dead lamb. I had only worked with machinery back in Ireland and I moved here to work for a big contractor. There wasn't a lot of work back home."

He continued.

"When I met Helen and moved here it was lambing season. They had one born ill; it couldn't stand. Helen's dad asked me to go out back and shoot it. I didn't want to, I didn't want to kill anything. Not even the hardest farmer can say they feel nothing when they have to shoot an animal. But I carried it out to the field and pointed the gun at it. I closed my eyes and shot it. I put it out of its pain and, if I hadn't, then Helen's dad would have.

"I thought about it for days after but, eventually, it got easier. You accept they don't all make it. I'm sorry Emily, I know it must seem like I'm being cold but unfortunately you can't control nature. After farming for as long as I have you just learn to accept it. Farming is tough. The toughest job. But you just have to think about all the ones that do make it and get turned out into the valley in the summer."

He raised his arm and looped the other around the lamb's belly so he was holding it like he might a cat. He turned and carried on walking.

Emily didn't know what to say, so she just followed him. He put the lamb down out the front of the cattle shed on the hay. They walked towards the house silently and went inside. Rome went to the sink to wash his hands. Emily pulled off her coat. The dogs lolloped over and hovered around Rome's legs. He stroked them with wet hands and then dried them on a tea towel. Emily watched as he took off his coat and hung it over the back of a chair and took off his buttoned-up shirt, leaving just a t-shirt underneath. The chain with the wedding rings was exposed on the white cotton. Emily watched him tuck them swiftly under his top. He threw his shirt out in the entry hall and then flicked the kettle on.

"What were you doing out there, anyway?" he asked. He wasn't looking at her. He had his back turned reaching for two mugs as Emily washed her hands.

"I couldn't sleep," she said. Rome didn't answer as he grabbed a teaspoon and started making the tea and coffee. He came over to the kitchen table and handed her a mug.

She sat for a few moments in silence and sipped it.

"I'm sorry about earlier. I shouldn't have questioned you about Georgina when it's none of my business," she said. She watched Rome's face fall.

"Don't worry about it," he replied.

"No, it's not my business. I just can't help myself sometimes. Mum always said I was too nosy for my own good."

Rome's eyebrows raised a millimetre and he took a sip of his coffee. She found her eyes had fixed themselves to his soft, Cupid's bow lips.

"It's all a pretty big mess," he said. She tore her eyes away.

"What if you marry her, assuming you don't love her, and fall in love for real with someone else?" she asked. She watched his face as he blinked and she noticed his long black eyelashes. His dark, blue eyes.

"I'm not going to fall in love," he said, simply. Emily sipped her tea. She held her hand out for Tess as she wound her way out from behind the table leg.

"I loved Helen, and she's gone. I won't love anyone else, I know it. I just don't think I'm capable of love anymore and honestly the only thing I care about is saving the farm."

"You're still grieving and I don't think you're thinking clearly, Rome. What if you're just feeling depressed? Eventually you'll start to care again and then you might regret your marriage to Georgina," Emily said, tentatively.

He looked at her, his expression a little darker. "Excuse me, Emily, but you don't exactly know me."

He was right, but she felt as though she did now. They hadn't known each other long but when you were living and working with someone all day long you got to know them pretty fast.

"And excuse me for saying that I don't think you're being fair," Emily shot back. "Just because your heart is broken and you don't care anymore doesn't mean you can mess with someone else and break their heart too." Emily felt instant regret as the words escaped her mouth. She hadn't meant it to sound so harsh.

"I'm sorry," she said, straight after. "I–"

"Don't worry about it," he said, standing. "Like I said before, you don't know the whole story. I need to go to bed."

He put his mug in the sink and left the kitchen. She trailed upstairs to bed a few minutes later, certain she wouldn't sleep now.

*

Emily opened her eyes and squinted at the bright ray of sunlight sliding between the gap in the curtains. Her mind returned instantly to the conversation she and Rome had shared in the night. She had been rude. She had poked her nose in and insulted him after he'd taken her into his home. She burned with embarrassment at the thought of what she had said. But still a part of her stuck by the comment. How was he being fair?

Emily went to the bathroom. She splashed water over her face and patted it dry. She didn't want to go downstairs and face Rome. It was seven, so he'd be back in an hour or so from his morning jobs. She hadn't got up to go with him this morning.

Emily got dressed and went downstairs, hoping Rome would still be out, and prepared a bottle for the orphan lamb.

"Here you go lamby," she offered. The lamb was pacing by her feet, bleating and looking up at her. She sat down on the sofa and the lamb ran after her. She offered the bottle and the lamb latched straight on drinking fast and hungrily, bunting the bottle occasionally. Emily thought about what she might say to Rome when they saw each other today. She didn't know if she should apologise or just let it go.

One thing was for sure, she wouldn't be bringing up the topic again. It was his life, his choice. She reminded herself sternly that she was here because of her own stupid mistake: falling into a trap with Mark. She was here because she needed a place to stay and Rome needed another pair of hands. She wasn't here to give him relationship therapy. She wasn't here to stick her nose in and she wasn't here to save him. She thought instead about the poor little lamb she couldn't save last night. She tried not to blame herself but couldn't help thinking there might have been more she could have done. Emily looked down at the lamb and noticed her chipped, once neatly manicured nails. She couldn't say she minded. She was glad not to have to keep such high standards now, not to be constantly worried about how she looked. Here, she could be herself at least.

The lamb had a full, round belly as it toddled off back to the carpet to lie down.

"No, come on you. Outside for the toilet." Emily had been taking the lamb out to the garden along with Rome's dogs so there wasn't so much mess to clean up indoors. She wasn't sure if it was possible to toilet train a lamb but she was giving it a go. They went out through the French doors to the conservatory and then out in the overgrown garden.

"Good girls," she said to Birdie and Tess, as they followed her out. They wagged their tails and tore across the lawn with each other, swirling around and chasing. Their fur glistened in the early morning sunlight. Emily could already see it was going to be another hot day. The light scent of honeysuckle drifted by as she looked across the garden and saw Seth's cottage a way down over the hedge row.

She thought about the orchard. She had been a little put off going there since Seth had told her it was Helen's. She felt as though she was treading on sacred ground, but surely she was doing a nice thing in tidying her orchard up? She didn't know Helen, but wouldn't she be happy if she knew someone was keeping her trees healthy?

She whistled the dogs inside and the little lamb bleated and trotted in after them. Birdie and Tess bundled into the kitchen with their tongues lolloping as they panted. They lapped up water from their bowl. Emily grabbed herself a glass from the tap, drank it and then headed for the back door.

*

Emily arrived in the orchard and closed the wooden gate behind her. She was completely hidden by the tall encircling hedges. It felt so secret and peaceful. She couldn't think of a place in the world that felt more calming.

Emily had found a pair of shears and an extended hooking device which she thought would be good for the hedges and she set to work. She started with the worst of it: the blackthorn trees which were sprouting. Emily cut them at the bottom and stared to form a pile, which she assumed she could burn when she was done. The work was satisfying as she took out the worst of the overgrown flora that shouldn't be there.

The sun rose higher in the sky and Emily took off her button-up shirt and tied it round her waist, wearing only her vest top. She trimmed and pulled and piled. She sweated and swore a few times as she spiked herself with the thorns. One particular baby blackthorn tree put up a real fight. Emily tugged at it with the cutters, but fell back onto one of the little trees she'd already pulled out. She cursed and staggered to her feet. That hurt. The tree had stabbed into the side of her leg, leaving a thorn which had snapped off, still embedded and sticking out from her jeans. She gingerly pulled it out and winced as it came free. She dropped it and turned her leg to inspect it. She couldn't really see but she could make out a little spot of red where the thorn had drawn blood.

Maybe she should call it a day. She'd made a good start on the hedges. The worst weeds were out. It was really only trimming that needed doing now. She looked at her phone, it was already eleven. She had been out here for over three hours.

Emily hoped Rome wouldn't ask questions as she walked back to the house. She wasn't sure she should tell him she had been in the orchard. Emily didn't want to cause any more unnecessary tension between them. Maybe she would wait until it was done and then show him. Or maybe that was insensitive and she would upset him. Maybe she wouldn't tell anyone and would just enjoy her project, knowing she was doing something nice in memory of Helen.

Emily walked into the kitchen of the farmhouse, where Rome was leaning against the sideboard, drinking coffee. The radio was playing quietly in the background. She gave him a fleeting smile as she passed and made her way through the living room to the door which led to the bigger sitting room and the staircase.

"What have you been up to?" he asked, stopping her in her tracks.

"I was just out walking," she lied. "You didn't need me for anything did you?"

"No it's all been quiet," he said. "I didn't mean to disturb you. Go, do whatever you were doing." He gave her a quick smile and then he left out the back door, heading for the farmyard.

Emily let out a long sigh. She wished she hadn't made things awkward.

Rome

Rome was in the living room slumped deeply on the cushioned sofa. The night was warm and he had the French doors open, leading out into the conservatory. The conservatory doors were open as well, letting the night air seep in. He loved the smell of night air, the faint scent of wild honeysuckle drifting in from the garden.

He was lost in thought when Emily walked in. She smiled at him quickly as she headed over to the kitchen fridge and rummaged. The dogs were lying lazily on the cool wooden floor and the lamb was next them. That reminded Rome, he had to settle it back outside soon; it couldn't live indoors forever. It was strong now and could fend for itself in the flock. They would just have to take a bottle for it outside. He was sure they'd have some more orphans soon enough. He'd managed to pair some with different mothers who had lost their lambs but it was tricky and it didn't always promise good results.

Emily crossed to the kitchen table and sat down with one of her natural yoghurts. Rome had tasted one the other day. He'd regretted it as soon as the yoghurt had made contact with his mouth.

"The lamb will have to go back out soon. Probably tomorrow," he said. He hoped she would understand it was in the lamb's best interests and not because he was trying to be awkward. It had been a few days since the night they'd lost a lamb. He didn't want things to be awkward. He didn't have the energy for it.

"Okay," she replied. She didn't seem too happy but wasn't devastated either. They didn't say anything as Emily finished off her yoghurt. From the corner of his eye he saw her stand up and wince as she touched her leg.

"What's up?" he asked, his eyes narrowing in concern.

"Oh nothing. Just my leg really hurts. I got a thorn in it when I went out walking the other day and it still hurts for some reason," she said, as she dropped her yoghurt pot in the bin.

"You probably still have a bit stuck in there. Do you want me to look?" he offered. He saw her hesitate. He felt the awkwardness as she looked at him.

"It's here," she said, indicating with her finger. She pointed to her upper leg, round by her bum.

"Not like I haven't seen a woman's ass before," he said, trying to make light of it, but she didn't smile. "Anyway, I've seen you naked in the shower haven't I?"

He laughed then, feeling the atmosphere lightening.

Her mouth opened as she gasped.

"I knew you saw," she wailed, and put her hands over her reddening face.

"Oh, come on. It doesn't matter," he smirked.

"It *does* really hurt. And I *am* wearing knickers this time," she said. Rome raised his eyebrows.

"Come over here then," he said, not getting up. He watched as she walked over and stood awkwardly before him. She turned her back to him and grabbed the waist band of her navy blue pyjama bottoms. He ignored the flicker which arose in his stomach. He saw her look back at his face before lowering the waist band down to the back of her upper thigh. He cleared his throat. There was a nasty swollen patch and a little pin hole where the thorn had gone in. It was red and that was a bad sign. He looked a little closer and didn't let his eyes rise. He wasn't looking at the black, lacy frill running across her pale skin. Emily pulled her waist band back up and turned around to face him.

"So?" she said. He felt heat rise in his cheeks. It had been a long time since he'd actually found pleasure looking at a woman's body. He didn't think he could feel that anymore.

"I think some is probably still stuck in there. I'll have to have a proper look," he said, noting Emily's horrified expression.

"Won't it just come out on its own?" she asked.

"I doubt it and, if you leave it any longer, you'll get an infection. Then you'll need antibiotics," he said. She looked worried. "But you'll be fine because I'll just get it out now. I'll just get a needle and some tweezers." He hauled himself up off the sofa and retrieved the first aid box from the medicine cabinet. The small bottle of whisky glinted at him from the top corner. He shut the door on it. He washed his hands at the sink and walked back over to Emily who was stood frozen on the spot in the middle of the room.

"You'll be fine. I've taken plenty out before," he promised, as he gave her a reassuring smile. "It'll probably be easier if you just lie on the sofa; that way you'll be still and I won't stab you too hard with the needle." He watched Emily turn pale. "I'm joking."

"Are you sure you want to do it?" she said.

"You're not going to make me drive you to hospital for a splinter are you?" he asked with a laugh. "I can do it."

She sighed and then rubbed her face with her hands. Groaning, she laid down on her front on the sofa. She tugged down her pyjama bottoms on the bad side and then pulled her hoody down lower over her bum. He didn't mean to stare, and didn't even know he was doing it until she cleared her throat.

"Sorry. It's been a while since I've had a naked woman on the sofa," he laughed.

"I'm hardly naked," Emily said, burying her face in the sofa cushion and holding her hands around the top of her head. He unzipped the first aid kit, taking out new tweezers and a needle from a packet, then took out an antiseptic wipe.

"I'm just going to clean it, okay?" he said.

"Uh huh." It came out muffled as her face was buried deep in the sofa cushion. He took the wipe from the packet and gently wiped it over the red surface, being careful not to let his fingers brush her leg. It was just a leg. He really shouldn't be enjoying it.

"Have you got your phone for a torch?" he asked. Emily rummaged in her pocket and pulled it out from underneath her. She handed it to him and he stared blankly at the screen.

"I actually can't do this," he said.

"Oh. Don't worry about it."

"Oh no, I'm getting it out of you. I mean the torch; I can't turn it on."

"Oh, I see." She laughed and took it, flicking the screen up and turning it on. He held it over her upper leg and inspected the area. He leant in close and could make out the faint black spot of a bit of thorn that was still stuck in there.

"I see it," he said. He picked up the needle and hovered the lighter flame over the end. He moved his free hand towards her leg and hesitated a little before gently touching her skin next to the thorn.

"I'm just going to go under the surface of the skin with the needle and flick it out. I can see it right there," he said to her.

"Be careful," she replied. Her eyes were scrunched shut and she was gritting her teeth.

"Don't be a wuss." Rome carefully placed the needle above the thorn and broke the surface of the skin to reach it.

"Okay?" he checked.

"Yeah."

He got the tweezers and managed to grab the end, gently pulling it out. She sucked air in through her teeth.

"Out," he announced, and held the tweezers in front of her face so she could see the thorn. She breathed out.

"It wasn't so bad. Thanks."

"No problem." He reached into the first aid box and took out the antiseptic. He rubbed it onto the clean pad on a plaster and carefully smoothed it on. "Just leave that on for a bit so you don't get cream all over your clothes."

"Okay. All done?" she asked.

"Yeah, all done." He got to his knees and put all the bits back in the box as Emily sat up awkwardly on the sofa.

"So, you're pretty accident prone," he said, with a laugh.

Emily smiled. "Seems that way, doesn't it? I guess I'm just bubble wrapped by city life where there are no cows, thorns and streams."

"Yeah." He looked up at her. She was leaning forward and he hadn't realised how close they were until now. He willed his eyes to stay locked on hers. He wasn't going to look at her lips. He focused on her radiant, blue eyes. They were lighter than his, like the summer sky.

They didn't speak. He knew they had stayed still too long. He knew it was turning into a moment. If he didn't look away now he would land himself in a whole load of trouble. As his eyes trailed lower he watched as her lips parted ever so slightly and it sent a tingle through his stomach.

"Sorry," he breathed. He averted his eyes and stood up quickly, rushing back to the kitchen to put the first aid kit away. He had his back to her and she was silent for what seemed like a long time. He heard a shuffle behind him and then she spoke.

"I guess I'll get off to bed then. Thanks for that."

He didn't look back. Rome didn't want to look at her. He was an idiot letting his guard down like that. He needed to stay cool. It wouldn't happen again.

"Night," he said, as he heard her walk away. He heard her footsteps on the stairs. Rome grabbed the kitchen counter with both hands and lowered his head as he let out a sigh. His feelings were churning around in his stomach. He didn't know what he felt anymore. There was no way he could let himself fall. He didn't even know he could feel emotions like that now, not after Helen. He was going to marry Georgina and that was final. That marriage *wouldn't* include an affair with Emily.

Emily

Emily jumped into bed and pulled the covers up to her chin. The coolness of the sheets made her shudder. She breathed deeply. That had been too much. She could still feel the gentle touch of his rough hand brushing against her leg. It had been nothing. He'd only been helping her out, so why did it feel like more to her? Was it hypocritical to think his relationship with Georgina was awful because of his grief for his wife, but actually like him herself?

When he had stared at her she had looked into his eyes and she was certain he was going to kiss her. He hadn't and he definitely seemed to regret the moment afterwards. The reality of Rome's engagement dawned on her and she knew now for sure she didn't want them to get married; not only for Georgina's sake. She hadn't known what real lust felt like until now. She had fancied men before, she had experienced plenty of teenage crushes years ago before she had settled down with Mark, but this was so different. She was beginning to yearn for him and it had happened so fast. The decent thing to do would be to move out and go to her mother's, but, more than anything, she wanted to stay.

*

The next morning, Emily and Rome were outside doing the morning feed. After Emily had gone to bed Rome had come to fetch her before she'd had a chance to sleep. They had spent the night in the lambing barn tending the sheep. There had been eight new lambs in the night. Neither of them had slept, apart from a half-hour's nap at five o'clock in the morning, on the straw, leant up against the wall of the barn. Emily could almost look back at her old life and laugh now. How different things had been. She had changed so much. Even looking down at her clothes it was evident. After what felt like the longest night in history they headed indoors for tea and coffee.

They went straight to the kitchen and were met with the welcoming sight of Georgina Dawson sat at the kitchen table.

"Georgina," said Rome, rubbing his eyes.

"Darling. I brought over some ingredients so we can have breakfast together," she said.

"Great, thanks," he replied, as he washed his hands, but somehow it didn't sound like he was pleased. Emily didn't say anything. She wasn't sure if she was invited to have breakfast with them or if Georgina had meant it as a couple's thing. Emily washed her hands when Rome was done and Georgina stood up and poured the last of her tea down the sink next to her. She started rummaging through a bag and took out the ingredients for a full English.

"I'll give you a hand," Rome said to her.

"Why don't you empty that bottle of juice into a jug and set the table? And please get the dogs out of the kitchen," Georgina said. Emily saw Rome's face tighten but he did as she asked and then gestured to a chair for Emily who was standing awkwardly by the sink.

"Take a seat, Emily," he said. Emily saw Georgina turn her head to eye Rome up but she didn't say anything.

Five minutes later the three of them were sat awkwardly round the table and no one had spoken much.

"Thank you so much for this, it looks lovely," Emily said to Georgina.

"Let me pour you some juice." Georgina gave Emily a tight lipped smile and grasped the juice with her left hand, when it would have clearly been easier to use her right. She leant across Rome and poured orange juice into Emily's glass. Her engagement ring glinted on her finger. The small, silver, jewelled ring fit her slim finger perfectly.

"Thank you," Emily said. They ate in silence for a while longer before Georgina piped up.

"When are you going to get that lamb out of the house, Rome? It must be using your living room as a toilet." Georgina looked distastefully at the little white lamb, which was lying peacefully on the rug with Birdie and Tess.

"Emily has been taking it out in the garden with the dogs, actually. It works fine. I'm thinking of reintroducing it to the flock but I haven't decided yet," Rome said, as he speared a mushroom onto his fork. Emily couldn't help but feel a small pang of happiness that he might have changed his mind about the lamb living indoors.

"I see. I think you should let the cleaner come down here. You haven't dusted in a long time. I'm sure Daddy won't mind if you borrow her," Georgina suggested.

"Perhaps." Rome seemed extremely uninterested in the topic of cleaning as he stood up to take his empty plate to the sink. He made a coffee while Emily continued to eat opposite Georgina.

"So how do you like Rome's house?" Georgina asked her. Emily hadn't been ready for her to speak and she quickly swallowed her mouthful while thinking up a response that wouldn't provoke Georgina to become angry or jealous.

"It has really lovely views out to the valley. It's very peaceful; I like it," she said. Emily felt nerves prickle in her stomach. Georgina clearly didn't like her.

"Yes, nice views. Has Rome taken you to the top of the valley?" she asked and then raised her glass to her red lips.

"No. I went up there myself to find a phone signal but we haven't been on any walks. It's really just silage and sheep afterbirth that make up our day," Emily said. Georgina raised a perfectly tweezed eyebrow. She was clearly fishing for dirt. Rome came back to the table in the nick of time and Emily could breathe again.

They finished off breakfast and Georgina made a show of kissing Rome at the door before leaving. She told him she was going riding but that she'd see him later and with a suggestive wink she kissed him again and left. Emily washed the dishes by the sink as Rome came back into the kitchen.

"I'm glad we can have a breakfast with no awkwardness," he said, as he rubbed his forehead. Emily sniggered and cleared her throat.

"It was just *lovely*."

Rome

Georgina had been swarming around Rome for the last few days like a bear around a bees' nest. He tried his best to act cheerful around her. She insisted on doing jobs with him like feeding the cows and checking the sheep. She had been hacking over in the early morning, as the sun was rising, to catch him while he was out working. Emily would always graciously make herself scarce and Rome was grateful for it. The last thing he wanted was tension between himself and Georgina.

Rome's thoughts were disturbed by the sheep in front of him. There weren't many to go now. He was hoping it would all go well so that he could turn them out soon. He heard Emily clink the metal gate shut as she came in the lambing barn to join him. She sat down beside him as he worked on the sheep.

"How's it looking?" she asked him.

"It's a big one," he said. He grunted as he pulled. They sat out in the dimly lit barn in silence. The sun had set an hour ago and dark clouds had moved in. Rome suspected that it would rain. The air felt heavy and was laced with the subtle scent of earthy sweetness. He was starting to sweat in the mugginess of the night as he gave the lamb another pull. It finally slipped out on the floor and lifted its head.

"It's huge," remarked Emily. Rome was happy to be around her again. She was easy company. He felt charged and stressed when he was around Georgina, but with Emily he could just be himself. They finished up in the barn and started walking up the yard towards the farmhouse just as the first fat raindrops began to fall. The rain fell heavy and they broke into a jog towards the house. Rome heard Emily squeal as a torrent came down and drenched them. She wrapped her sodden cardigan around her. The water soaked through Rome's clothes and touched his skin. They made it to the top of the yard.

"Quick," he said. They raced through the garden gate and through the back door, into the outhouse. The rain pounded the roof of the outhouse like galloping horses on a race track. They stumbled through to the kitchen and Emily turned to him, laughing.

"What was that?" she shrieked, holding out her arms and looking down at her water laden clothes.

"April showers," he said, as he peeled his hoody off over his head.

"It's May," said Emily, taking off her drenched cardigan and holding it at arm's length before her. Rome went to the sink to wash his hands. He dried them and raked a hand through his soaked hair to push it out of his eyes.

"I'm freezing," she said to him. He watched her blond hair dripping onto the floor, droplets of rainwater falling down her face.

"Go and have a bath," he said.

"What about you? You must be cold too," she said.

The thought crossed his mind of what it would be like to share a bath with Emily, but he forced it away.

"I'll be fine, I'll go dry off," he assured her. They headed upstairs together and Rome went to the airing cupboard to take out two large, soft towels. He passed one to Emily.

"Thanks. I'll go run a bath."

Rome went to his bedroom and stripped off. He towelled his body dry and put on a clean hoody and jeans. As he was drying his hair he heard a scream from the bathroom. His heart lurched and he bolted from his room. He pushed the bathroom door open without a second's thought and Emily caught her bath towel up against her body.

"What's wrong?" he demanded.

"That's the second time you've burst in on me," she said. "There is the hugest spider in the bath."

He held a hand to his chest. "You can't scream like that; I thought you'd fallen over."

"Sorry. Can you get it out?" she asked, as she hoisted her bath towel higher.

"Sure." He reached in and caught the spider in cupped hands. Emily eyed him wearily and backed away as he opened the window and put it outside.

"It will drown in the rain now," she said.

"You wanted me to get it," he replied with a laugh. He stared at her in silence. She bent to put the plug in the bath and turn on the taps. Steam rose from the bubbling water like a cauldron. Emily turned to face him.

"Planning on joining me?" she asked, joking casually.

"Sorry," he said, embarrassed. She was obviously hinting that he should leave. The pull to stay was strong as their eyes locked. He traced his gaze over her; he couldn't help but find her sexy with her wet hair clinging to her damp skin. He felt instant betrayal and guilt for Helen. He had never found anyone else attractive since her, certainly not Georgina.

Rome had stayed in the bathroom too long now and he knew it. It had gone past the point of appropriateness. She wasn't breaking eye contact either. Did she find him attractive too?

"So you really are joining me then?" She said it more seriously this time and it sent a wave of longing through his stomach. The emotions were so mixed. He felt guilt most prominently but also anger that he and Seth couldn't afford their farm so he was having to give himself to Georgina. Rome raked a hand firmly through his hair. He hadn't had many regrets about the plan so far apart from the obvious guilt about marrying another woman. This was the first moment he had doubted if he could manage it. Even so, Rome knew he had to stick with the plan or he would lose everything that mattered to him.

But maybe the farm wasn't all that mattered now. Maybe it was time to admit that he was beginning to feel alive again. If he married Georgina it meant he was losing any hope of having the woman standing in front of him. He couldn't hold Emily and kiss her. He couldn't let her comfort him or let her be anything more than a helping hand on the farm. He took a step closer. Emily didn't back away. It was like his mind was clouded, like he couldn't see the terrible mistake looming because his brain was useless and his priorities were masked with lust. It was almost like a physical force was pulling him to her. Like there was nothing he could do to stop himself from reaching out to her. Even to touch the bare skin on her shoulder. He just needed some contact to stop the dizzying whirl in his head.

Emily held out her hand and touched his. She brought it from his side and held onto it, and the innocent gesture sent a shudder through his body. Rome wished he knew what she was thinking as she took a step towards him. He felt a buzz as if he were drunk as she looked up at him and traced the fingers of her free hand down his jawline. He leant into her touch, tipping his head forwards. Soft and delicate fingertips brushed against his rough stubble and he reached out his hand and grazed his thumb along her bottom lip. Perfectly soft.

He drew back sharply. His hand fell back by his side as something in him snapped and he stepped backwards, breaking the contact and putting distance between them. What was he doing? He had almost ruined everything.

"I'm so sorry," he said quietly and he swiftly left the bathroom closing the door behind him.

Emily

Emily stood listening to the water gush into the bath. The door had closed and he was gone. Her heart was hammering. Her hand was tingling from where it had grazed his face. Her mind whirled. She had thought she saw the signs, had thought he wanted her. She hadn't imagined the look of longing in his eyes. Either he didn't feel the same way and she had been way off or he had considered it and then regretted it and bailed. How silly of her, trying to make a move on the man whose house she was living in; the man who had let her stay here for free and been kind to her. He was engaged, certainly not for the right reasons, but engaged nonetheless. She wouldn't do it again. There had been too many moments, too many looks, too much suggestion, too much touching.

Rome didn't speak about their moment until Emily brought it up the next morning. He was out by the sheep field with his dogs leaning against the wooden gate. She didn't want to drag it out.

"Rome?" She played nervously with her frayed sleeve. He looked over as she approached him, letting his hand slide off the gate as he turned to face her.

"What's up?" he asked, squinting in the morning sunlight. Emily thought about how best to word it.

"I wanted to say sorry for last night." She cleared her throat. "For what happened in the bathroom." She watched as Rome's cheeks reddened and his eyes flicked around unsure where to look. "Do you think it would be better if I left?" Emily waited for his answer. He seemed to be thinking about what she had just said.

"I don't want you to go Emily." He looked away from her then and back over towards the sheep grazing in the valley. "It's not like anyone needs to find out. We never did anything. I didn't cheat." He looked back at her then and she felt her face grow hotter.

"I suppose so."

"I think it would be much easier if we could just forget about it and not bring it up again."

Emily nodded.

The next few days were awkward. Emily felt as though each conversation between them was strained and scripted. She didn't feel as though they were themselves around each other anymore.

Emily

The last few sheep that were due to give birth had done so in the last few days. It had been a busy three weeks but they were finally done. Emily and Rome had managed to put their moment in the bathroom behind them and were pretty much back to normal. Emily had been at the farm almost a month now and it felt like home.

It was a sunny, warm day in May as she and Rome made their way down to the lambing shed to turn them out into the valley. Lambing was over and they were going back outside. Emily's orphan was trotting after them as they rounded the corner and arrived at the barn. She was going to be turned out with the rest. Emily was sorry to let her go but she had to be with the rest of the flock. Seth was waiting by the shed as Emily and Rome walked down towards him.

"All right," Rome greeted him.

"All right. Hi Emily," Seth replied.

"Finally, turn out time," said Rome, as he untied the baling twine on the gates to the shed.

"We didn't do too badly. We got a nice number of lambs; not too many died," said Seth, looking over the flock.

"Could have gone worse," agreed Rome.

"All right, let's get going." Rome untied the gates to the lambing shed. "If you want to go over and untie the field gate, Emily and I will herd them down."

"Full of orders now my leg's broke," Seth said laughing, as he made his way down to the field gates. Emily and Rome went in and released the last few lambs and ewes from their separate hurdle pens so they could join the main flock. Rome whistled to his dogs and they looped round the sheep to guide them out of the shed.

Rome was up the yard a little way making sure the sheep would run down to the field and not back towards the farmhouse. The sheep moved down towards the field and then as they reached the gateway they leaped and ran out into the grass. The lambs sprang into the air and Emily had never seen anything like it. All three of them stood with their arms dangling over the gate, watching as the sheep bounded down the valley towards the stream. Rome smiled.

"I love turn out," he said.

"They look so happy," said Emily.

They all stood in silence for a few minutes in the sunshine, marvelling at the view of the lower valley and beyond. Neighbouring fields looked sewn together with hedgerows, making a patchwork quilt of all shades of green. The spire of the village church was visible down below, just beyond the creek and over the trees. The sheep were little white dots now as they made their way further down and the lambs explored their new freedom. Emily could get used to the view from Bramblewood Farm.

"Are you going to the show then in a few weeks Rome?" Seth asked, breaking the silence.

"I suspect Georgina will force me to, don't you?" he said.

"It won't be too bad. I'll have my cast off, I'll be able to get around," Seth said.

"What show?" Emily asked, intrigued.

"Every year in June they hold a county show at Addleton Estate," Seth said. "The estate rents out a few big fields for the people who run it. Quite a lot of visitors go: most of the people from the village and loads from further away."

"What's it like then?" said Emily.

"People bring animals and show them. There's a cow tent, chicken tent and sheep tent. They have horse showing, tractors, food. It's great," said Seth. "You can come with me if you like. I don't have anyone to go with and you don't want to be lumbered with Rome and Georgina." He laughed, winking at Rome.

"Sounds good, thanks," Emily said.

"I'm sure I'll be stuck out by the horse lorries, helping with her every wish and command. She'll be showing them there," said Rome.

They turned and began walking back up the yard.

"How did you break your leg, then? I still don't know," Emily asked Seth.

"I was out checking the sheep before lambing started and I fell over the rocks in the stream."

Emily laughed. "Oh, I expected an action story."

"Nope, just sheer clumsiness," he said.

"I'm lucky my legs are intact then, looks like we've got something in common," she replied.

*

Later that day, Emily headed out to the orchard. She couldn't help but feel a slight sense of guilt as she walked through the gate. This was Helen's orchard and Emily knew that she was beginning to develop feelings for Helen's husband. She hoped Helen wouldn't mind her being there. She was helping the trees, after all.

Emily began snipping the brambles away from the trunks and piled them up on the stack of other things she'd torn from the ground. There were easily over one hundred trees, but Emily made a start. The more she tackled the better it looked. She really felt like she was achieving something. After spending a couple of hours tearing away the brambles she walked over to a shady corner underneath the tendrils of the weeping willow and sat to take in the view of what she had done. Emily noticed two strings of rope dangling from a branch where a swing must have once hung.

A pair of Canadian geese flew purposefully across the blue sky. Their wings beat hard and they called as they went. Robins, blackbirds and finches twittered at a high pitch in the surrounding hedgerows and their sweet sounds filled the atmosphere. The buzzing of bees thickened the air and, as Emily sat in the short grass admiring the view, she imagined herself in a fairy tale in a world hundreds of years ago, where there were no cars or big cities. Just countryside and simplistic life. Emily now understood what it was like to live just for life, not for money or social media. She couldn't imagine a place she would rather be than here, living off the land.

Rome

The days grew warmer as May swiftly turned to June. The grass turned a darker shade of green, the leaves of the oaks thickened the hedgerows and the air smelled of heat and warmth. It was the county show at Addleton Estate today. Georgina would already be up, faffing with her horses. Rome had been instructed when and where to meet her after he had finished the jobs. Emily didn't have so much to help him with now the flock was out but soon they would start the summer work of cutting the grass and haymaking. He was sure Emily would still be a big help, even now Seth's leg was better. He had gotten his cast removed a couple of days ago and had been taking it easy but he'd be in full swing again soon. He hadn't really thought about Emily's fate here once Seth was better. It had been a temporary arrangement while he needed extra help but surely she could stay.

Rome headed inside and changed into clean jeans and a smart button-up shirt. He headed down to the kitchen where Emily was cleaning up after breakfast.

"I need to get off," he said. "Georgina needs a hand."

"I'll be along later with Seth."

Rome drove through the country lanes until he reached the main road connecting the lower valley with Addleton Estate. He drove up the road and past the huge black gates which led to the grand driveway of the manor. He gazed up the drive through the closed gates at the big house as he drove by.

He reached the back entrance to the show where the horse lorries were allowed to park and drove in past the gate man. He spotted Georgina with a crowd of other women fretting over their horses. Parking up near them, he headed over towards Georgina's flash horse lorry. She had insisted on using it even though she could have led her horses over from the stables. She just wanted to show it off.

"Rome," she called, as he approached. He smiled in her direction. He saw the girls behind Georgina incline their heads and whisper. Horsey girls like that loved men and gossip even more than their horses. Georgina rushed over and took his arm. She led him over to the group of women.

"Girls, this is Rome, my fiancé." She thrust out her hand, pointing her ring at them.

"Very nice," one of them said. The other women giggled as they stood with their hands on their hips.

They all wore tight, beige riding breeches and white buttoned shirts.

"So, when is the wedding?" one of them asked.

"Oh, it will be this summer," Georgina replied. Rome almost choked on thin air. That was the first he'd heard of it. Georgina bustled him past the group of women over to the side of her lorry, where two horses were tied. She handed him a bottle of baby oil.

"Oil their noses, will you Rome? I don't want to get grease on my jodhpurs," she said. He took the bottle and approached the grey horse. He squirted oil into his hand and smoothed it over the horse's grey muzzle, then did the same to the chestnut.

"When are you going in the ring then?" he asked as he watched her rush around with some tack.

"The first class is in twenty minutes so I need to ride down there and warm up," she said. He nodded. Georgina lifted a saddle up onto the grey's back, buckled up the girth, then put on the bridle. She untied the horse from the lorry.

"Will you give me a leg up and lead me to the ring?" she said.

"Sure," Rome held out his hands and she lifted her shin into them as he hoisted her up. Georgina jerked the horse hard in the mouth as she yanked on the reins to turn it. He had never liked the way she was rough with her horses. Helen had always been so gentle when she rode Bramley. They used to hack down to the beach and she would let him paddle along the shoreline. He had been retired since the accident.

Rome led Georgina out of the first field into the main one. It was about thirty acres, filled with white marquees, show rings and food stalls. The show was already buzzing with activity but Rome knew it would get even more busy as the crowds arrived for their day out.

Emily

Emily and Seth arrived at the show and parked in the main car park. The sun was high in the sky and Emily was glad she had picked out a dress to wear. They walked through the gateway and were given a stamp on their hands so they could get back in. The field was huge. It was alive with people and animals. Emily tried to take it all in as they moved through the crowd. Was there even an organised way to walk round one of these events?

"What do you want to do first then?" asked Seth.

"I have no idea. What do you do at these things?" she asked.

"We could start with food?" he suggested.

"Sounds good." Emily put her sunglasses on as they walked away from the entrance. They passed some fairground rides, coconut shies and swing boats. They passed country dancers and a crowd of spectators.

"Wow," said Emily, as they reached the food hall. The tent was filled with different stands selling all sorts of homemade food: pork pies, fudge, cider, sausage rolls. Emily's stomach rumbled as they stood before a hot counter of handmade savoury pastries. They ordered warm sausage rolls, which Seth told her were the best she'd ever taste, and two pints of freshly squeezed apple juice, which they took outside to enjoy on the grass.

They had the view of the cattle show ring and Emily watched as large white cows were led round on halters.

"There Charolaise. Nice aren't they?" Seth said to her.

"Not as nice as this sausage roll. It's to die for." Emily's mouth was stuffed with buttery pastry as she took her third bite.

"Told you so," Seth laughed.

*

Before long, Emily and Seth were on the move again. They had looked around the cow tents and seen some sheep and pigs when Seth began to get fidgety.

"I'm really sorry, I'm going to have to go and find a toilet. That apple juice has hit me."

"I might go see if I can find Rome for a bit then. You can come and meet us after?" Emily suggested.

"Sure, I expect he'll be over by the horse ring," Seth said. He flashed a smile and blended into the crowd. Emily walked past a stand selling popcorn and candy floss. She couldn't help herself. She hadn't had candy floss since she was a little girl. She bought it on a stick and carried on down towards the horse ring. She pulled off pieces of fluffy pink sugar and let dissolve in her mouth as she neared the ring. People were gathered around watching a tall chestnut horse canter around, flying over jumps. Emily could never imagine herself being brave enough to do that.

She caught sight of Rome standing alone watching the horse as it sailed around the ring. He looked handsome in his clean buttoned shirt and dark jeans. He was wearing a black cowboy hat. His face was half hidden and she had struggled to pick him out of the crowd. He turned his head to look at her as she approached and she caught sight of a smile widening beneath the shadow cast across his face.

"Hey," he said, as she stood next to him.

"Hi."

"I see you found some candy floss."

"I couldn't believe it; I haven't had it for years. It's not as good I remember but I guess the thought of eating pink fluff makes the whole experience better when you're a kid."

"I bet. Where's Seth got to then?" he asked.

"He went to the loo; we had a lot of apple juice."

"I see. Georgina's in the ring." He cast his eyes back to the grey horse and its rider. Emily nodded.

"Rome Buckley. Are you enjoying the view of my daughter in the show ring?" A woman had approached Rome, touching him on the arm as she spoke. She was wearing a summer hat and a modest dress with a red show member's badge attached. She was refined and well-spoken.

"Hello, Isobelle. Yes, she looks grand in there doesn't she?"

Emily watched him tilt his hat up and give the woman a charming smile.

"I was happy to hear the news that you had proposed. Georgina deserves it," the woman said.

"She does," Rome replied.

"Lovely to see you.' She glanced briefly at Emily. 'I must be getting on, we are having tea in the members enclosure. I'm sure I will see you shortly. I know Georgina is already chomping at the bit to get the wedding plans underway." The woman gave a smile but her nose continued to point towards the sky, her chin ever so slightly jutting outwards conveying her refinement.

"See you soon," said Rome. The woman walked away and Rome's smile instantly faded. He tipped his hat back further over his eyes. Emily took a step closer to him.

"I assume that was Georgina's mother?"

"It was," he replied.

"So, how soon is the wedding going to be?"

"This summer, apparently. Not that I have a say," said Rome. Emily's heart skipped a little faster. This summer; it was so soon. A tiny part of Emily had thought it wouldn't go ahead but there clearly wasn't much time for it to be stopped.

Emily sighed and leant back against the fence of the show ring. Rome turned to look at her.

"Georgina is using me just the same as I am her," he said.

"What do you mean?"

"She has an older brother, Daniel, who is due to inherit majority control over the estate. They don't get on very well and she knows he'll push her out when their mother and father die. She knows if she marries me then she will be in charge of the farm and the valley. She will be securing her own stability and land. She wants the farm house and mine and Seth's farm much more than she wants me. I'm not her type at all. I'm sure she has no feelings for me whatsoever."

Emily couldn't help but wonder who wouldn't find Rome attractive.

"Why didn't you tell me this before? Not that it makes it much better but at least it means Georgina's heart isn't on the line," said Emily.

"I just don't like to talk about it. I'm not exactly proud of the whole situation: two people using each other for their own selfish reasons." Rome paused for a few moments, rubbing the stubble on his jawline. "She's clever you know. I have no doubt that she strongly suspects the only reason I'm marrying her is to keep the farm. She won't be able to charge me rent or kick me out once we're married and I will have the farm secured. Seth and I will be able to keep our home. This is going to benefit everyone." He looked down at the floor and scuffed his boot in the dusty ground.

"Why does she get so jealous of us living together if it's an act?" asked Emily, unconvinced by this sudden revelation.

"I expect she knows you're my type." Rome shifted uncomfortably, his eyes cast down. "She is probably afraid I'll develop feelings for you and break off the engagement. She gets what she wants; it's in her nature and she won't have this be any different. You just have to accept it Emily. We all just have to do what we must to survive."

Emily's heart had fluttered when he had called her his type but now all she felt was frustration. If Rome was telling the truth that Georgina didn't love him and Rome definitely didn't love her then was there hope? Rome seemed to read her expression.

"There's no other way Emily." He paused. "We thought we'd found a way round it once. Me and Seth. We were talking. It was a little like the conversation we're having now. We were looking through a box of old photos and thinking about Helen. We found a will written by Seth and Helen's dad. Seth and I spent hours poring over it, trying to figure out if it meant something. If there was even the slightest chance ..." Before Rome could finish the horse and rider exited the ring and rode out past Emily and Rome.

"Are you coming down to the lorries to help me, Rome?" Georgina called from atop her horse.

"Sorry," Rome said to Emily.

"Don't worry. Seth will be along soon," Emily said, as he turned and left. He took hold of the reins beneath the horse's neck as he led Georgina away leaving Emily's mind spinning, thinking about Rome and wills. What was he talking about?

Rome

Summer had melted upon them and the days had turned hot. The evenings were warm and light as they stretched into night. The cows were out grazing in the lower valley with the sheep. Georgina had been round a lot, planning the wedding. She had all sorts of questions about ceremonies, afterparties, flowers, food and rings. Rome would try and give an opinion but in the end she always decided anyway. The whole thing just didn't seem real.

Georgina wanted the wedding to be huge, of course. She had invited hundreds of people, most of whom Rome didn't know. She wanted the ceremony at the big house, since it was licenced for marriage and the reception in the ballroom, stretching out into the gardens. There was going to be fireworks and extravagant food. Rome felt way out of his depth with the whole thing. He couldn't think of anything worse than having to do this in front of a load of posh people he didn't know and then have to pretend he was happy afterwards as they ate crab and sipped champagne.

His wedding to Helen had been intimate and sweet. They had gotten married at the church in the village and then come back to the farm where they'd had a hog roast and Helen's homemade cider. It had been them and their families and some of their friends from the village. He didn't know how he would bear the day Georgina had planned.

Rome headed across the yard. So far it had been a Georgina free day. He spotted Emily leaving the house. She came towards him, smiling.

"I was looking at the garden a few days ago when I got back from the show and I was wondering if you would mind if I mowed it," she said.

Rome had stopped mowing the garden when Helen died. She used to love the garden. She would plant all sort of gorgeous flowers. The smells used to fill the house as they drifted through the conservatory.

"I don't mind, but we don't have a very good mower," he said.

"I actually have one," she said.

"You have a mower?" Rome's eyebrows crept up.

"Yep. Mark packed it up for me when he sent my stuff back."

"He gave you the *mower*?"

"Yes. He was petty about it all. Kept everything he paid for and gave me everything I paid for."

"You lived in a flat," said Rome.

"There was a garden round the back that we owned. I used to mow it," said Emily.

"Okay, go for it," he replied. She smiled and walked away, towards the back of the house. Where had she been keeping her mower all this time? Would he ever stop being surprised by her?

*

A few weeks later, Rome was out checking the baled hay in the upper fields. There was only one tractor load today. He was sure there would be much more as the summer went on, it had just been hard with only him and Seth. With the wedding coming up he didn't want too much hay on the ground that he wouldn't have time to bale and store away in the shed. Now he just needed some help to get the bales stacked on the tractor so they could get them into the barn. He had enlisted Seth, but he wondered if Emily might be able to help as well.

He walked through to the kitchen but there was no sign of Emily.

"Emily?"

Rome walked through the sitting room and peaked through the door into the lounge. He called upstairs a little louder this time.

"Emily?"

He went back to the sitting room and then a faint buzzing sound drew him towards the conservatory. The hum of an engine led him out into the garden. Rome's eyes widened at the sight before him. She had almost finished mowing the whole lawn. It was still a bit rough and it needed strimming round the edges but it took him back in time. The last time he had seen the garden like this was before Helen had died. Seeing Emily push the mower through the wispy grass was like seeing Helen's ghost. Just then she caught his eye and turned off the mower. She came over, smiling.

"What do you think?" she said.

"It looks really good. Just how Helen used to have it," he said. "Could you give me a hand to get the bales in? I need us both up on the trailer. Is that okay?"

"Sure. I'll run inside and grab a drink, then we'll go." As she passed him, the scents of honeysuckle and cut grass drifted by, carrying with them the memory of Helen and the jolt of pain that always followed.

Rome and Emily left through the back door and headed across the yard. Rome began to explain fully to Emily how it would all work.

"Seth will be in the tractor and he'll use the bale grab to go round and pick the bales up off the ground." Rome painted a picture using his hands to imitate the tractor loader as they walked through the gate and headed towards the upper valley. "He'll put them on the trailer and then you and I just have to arrange them so the stack stays steady and strong. There's a special way they go on the trailer but I'll show you that. All good?" he said.

Emily nodded. "I'll give it a go."

Emily

Emily hadn't told Rome she was already exhausted from hacking down the overgrown lawn behind the farmhouse as they started to work in the field. She would just have to push on. This was farming, after all.

Emily and Rome climbed onto the trailer and watched as Seth got up into the tractor. He drove over to the first cluster of eight bales and used the square grab on the front of the loader to pick them up with the spikes protruding from the grab. He drove them over to the trailer and lowered them down. The spikes in the bales retracted and they dropped onto the trailer.

"We just have to put them in the right place. We need a row of horizontal bales on the left and another on the right. Then we'll have a vertical line down the middle." Rome called over the rumble of the tractor engine. "On the next layer we will have the vertical line on the left and the horizontal lines on the right and in the middle. Then we just alternate so the vertical line switches between the left and right as we go up a layer." He said it breezily, but Emily was utterly confused and it clearly showed on her face.

"Just copy me," he said, and began to move the bales around. He arranged two horizontal lines on the left and right and then put the rest down the middle. Before she knew it Seth was back with another eight. Seth dumped them onto the trailer and Emily grabbed one by the strings to continue Rome's pattern. By the time she had moved three he had already put the other five into place. The bales were much heavier than she expected them to be. They moved up a layer so they were now standing on the bales they had already put in place.

"Now the vertical line goes down the left. It's the most important one, and we need to get straight edges, otherwise the stack could fall," Rome said.

"Yep."

Another load of bales came and Emily put the horizontal ones in place while Rome created the straight line. Before Emily knew it they were seven layers high. She got onto her hands and knees and peeked over the edge. They were high.

"How many layers go on a trailer then?" she asked Rome as she stood back up. She watched as sweat dripped down his face and off his nose. He was wearing a faded tank top and jeans, the top showing off his biceps.

"About ten layers. Why, are you scared of heights?" he asked.

"No," said Emily, although looking down at the ground below was terrifying her. She couldn't imagine being ten layers high. Rome walked towards the back of the trailer as another eight were put on by Seth. As he walked behind Emily he grabbed her by the waist and pushed her towards the edge, pretending to drop her. He didn't let go as he grabbed her back towards him. Emily screamed.

"You idiot!" she shouted, with her hand to her heart, but she was laughing soon enough.

"It's character building," he said, laughing, as he grabbed hold of a bale. Emily watched the muscles in his arms strain as he put it into the jigsaw on top of the rest.

They reached the ten layer mark and there were no bales left in the field. Emily slouched down on top of the hay and took a breath. She sweated like she never had before. She thought she had worked hard when she had mowed the orchard with the push along mower but this was another level. The sun was burning down on them and she felt dizzy with exhaustion and heat. She couldn't deny, though, that the view from the top was the most spectacular one she had ever seen. The valley rolled below them and she could see way down to the farmhouse. Even the tips of the orchard trees were visible. She could see the creek far beyond and sheep dotted in the lower pastures. She could even make out the church spire of the little village. Beyond that was the horizon, blurred slightly by the heat of the sun. A thought suddenly dawned on her as she watched Rome stand by the edge.

"How are we getting down from here?" she asked, feeling unsteady as she peered down. Rome turned to her and smiled. Emily felt her stomach churn. "Seriously, how are we getting down?"

Seth drove over to the stack with the bale grab lifted in the air. There were no bales on it as he lifted it up and hovered it at the very top of the stack over the tenth layer.

"Ready to get down?" Seth stuck his head out of the open tractor door as he called to them. The tractor loader was stretched to its full height. Emily looked at Rome.

"No." She shook her head.

"Come on, it's fun. This is the best bit." He smiled daringly. Emily was petrified.

"There must be another way down," she insisted.

"Oh yeah, of course, there is another way."

"What?" she asked hopefully, getting steadily to her feet.

"You could jump," he said, with a laugh.

"Very funny," she replied. "If I had known this was going to be part of the deal I would never have built myself up here."

"You'll be fine, I promise." Rome offered his hand to her. She looked at it hesitantly and took it. He led her to the edge. He sat precariously on top of the scary looking metal contraption.

"This can't be how you're meant to do it. What about health and safety?"

"This is farming Emily. We don't actually care that much about health and safety," he laughed. Emily closed her eyes and took a deep breath. She grabbed Rome's hand harder as she stepped towards the edge. She reached out with her free hand and grabbed hold of the metal bale grab. She perched on the edge of it, holding Rome's hand in a death grip in one hand and the metal of the grab in the other.

"You on properly?" he asked.

"Yes, let's just do it," she said, as she squeezed her eyes shut. The grab began to lift and Emily kept her eyes scrunched shut. She felt them go backwards and then lower to the ground.

"You can open your eyes now," Rome laughed. Emily scrambled off and stood up straight on the hard floor. It felt strange to be down low again. She felt heavier and more stable. She looked up at the tall stack, feeling tiny and short.

"I can't believe I was just up there."

"You did great. Thanks for your help," said Rome.

Emily watched as Seth hitched up the trailer and drove the stack down towards the farmyard. Rome began to walk after it and she followed.

"Helen used to bring us cold cider when we were doing bale cart. It was the best after you had spent hours sweating in the heat," Rome said. Emily watched him gaze into the distance.

"I bet that was nice."

"I just can't believe the wedding is tomorrow." Rome raked a hand through his damp, dark hair. Emily's heart twinged. She had spent most of the morning thinking about it. Georgina hadn't been seen for a few days. She was obviously busy overseeing the wedding set up at the big house.

"So, is everything ready then?" Emily asked.

"Georgina is bringing my suit up tonight. It had alterations in the week. I guess she has it all sorted. I went up there a few days ago and it was madness, there were people with clipboards everywhere. I left her to it. I just told her I was way too busy on the farm to be up there. Which I am," he said.

"So, you're definitely doing it?"

"Definitely," he said. "I can't stop thinking about Helen, though. What would she think of me? I'm trying to do what's best. She loved the farm and I just want to keep it for her."

"I'm sure Helen would just want you to do what makes you happy," Emily replied.

"Neither option can make me happy. I keep thinking about visiting her. Her ashes are scattered in the orchard. But I don't think I can. I feel like I've betrayed her."

Emily felt Goosebumps prickle over her body. Helen's ashes were in the orchard? She had completely overstepped the line going in there and invading it. How could she have known? Would Rome be furious? Should she tell him?

"You could always change your mind," Emily said, trying to focus on their conversation again.

"And then Seth and I lose the farm. I lose my animals and everything Helen's family and I worked for. I lose Helen and all of our memories."

Emily saw Rome wipe his eye. She reached out and rubbed her hand on his back.

"I don't know what to say."

"You will come to the wedding tomorrow, won't you?" he said.

"If you need me there," she said.

"Thank you."

He smiled at her. His smile was familiar to her now but still it made her heart flutter. Tomorrow he would be lost to her forever.

"Do you know what the best thing to do is after the bale cart?" he said. His voice was lighter now.

"You'll have to help me out with that one."

"Follow me," he said, as he broke into a jog.

"You're kidding. How can you run anywhere now?" she called after him. She tried to keep up as he flew down the valley. They passed the farmyard and carried on down through the grassland. They ran down the hill, towards the lower fields where the sheep were grazing, until they reached the river. Emily leant forwards, trying to catch her breath. As she rose she saw Rome reach his arms behind him and pull his shirt off over his head. His muscular body was coated in a sheen of sweat and it glistened, tanned and golden in the sun. He took off his jeans as if Emily weren't there and then he waded into the steam until he reached a deep part, where he dipped his head under and back up.

"Come in, it's the best," he said, as he pushed his hair back. Emily laughed.

"I'm not taking my clothes off," she said.

"That's the best bit about it. I'd do it naked if you weren't here," he replied. "Anyway, I've seen you naked."

"So you keep reminding me," she said. If only he knew what those kinds of jokes did to her insides.

Rome grinned as he laid back and floated in the stream. That grin got her every time.

Emily couldn't deny that the water looked nice. She was itching from the hay and it had stuck to the sweat on her body, so she took off her shorts, noticing how scratched her legs were from picking up the hay. That would be why Rome had worn jeans in twenty degree heat. She stepped out of her shorts and pulled off her t-shirt. It was just the same as wearing a bikini, she assured herself.

Emily quickly waded in before Rome caught sight of her. The water was cool and made her gasp as she lowered in up to her shoulders, but it was so refreshing. The water trickled gently downwards towards the creek at the bottom of the valley. It was clear and Emily could see her feet touching the rocks below her. The sheep and cattle were grazing not far away. It was perfect after a hard day's work.

Looking at the crystal clear water made Emily realise how dry her mouth was.

"Thirsty?" Rome was watching her as she gazed at the water. "Just drink from the stream," he said, taking a gulp full.

"Rome, I don't think you're supposed to drink that," she said.

"Sure you are, it's fine. The sheep drink it. It's running water from way up in the hills. It's fresh." Emily gave him a wary look. "You won't taste better water."

"Are you sure it's safe?" she asked. He took another gulp to prove it. She lowered her face to the stream and sipped a mouthful of water. It did taste good. It was earthy and fresh. She took a few more sips. She didn't want to drink too much, just in case.

"It's all right," she confirmed. "I feel like a real farmer now, bathing in the stream."

"You already did it once when you fell in that time," he pointed out, with a laugh.

"Thanks for reminding me," she said. They floated around in silence for a while and admired the view before Emily spoke. "So what time is the wedding starting tomorrow then?"

"Georgina printed me out a whole schedule of when I'm supposed to be there and what I'm meant to say and where I'm meant to stand," he said.

"That sounds very specific."

"I think the guests are arriving at elevenish or something like that. Then we're having the ceremony in the house and the reception in the ballroom.' He looked up at Emily. 'It leads out onto the gardens. It's a nice spot.' He added quietly, looking away.

Emily had to admit it sounded pretty nice. "I see."

"Let's not talk about it anyway. I don't want to think about it anymore than I have to," Emily noticed the way he pulled in his lower lip, biting it gently and prompting a flutter in her stomach. His eyes were downcast as he gazed into the rippling water.

"Sure." Emily flicked up some water and splashed him. He laughed and splashed her back.

"Don't start what you can't finish," he warned her, eyes sparkling.

She flicked some more.

"Don't say I didn't warn you."

He came towards her and ducked down, grabbing her around her upper thighs. He picked her up effortlessly and deposited her down into the water. She went fully under and pushed herself back up. She laughed as she flicked her loose hair back. They looked at each other. Emily couldn't deny how handsome he was, tanned and dripping wet. His dark hair was pushed back. His eyes twinkled playfully. She moved towards him and jumped to grab his shoulders and push him down. He didn't move. He looked amused.

"Were you trying to dunk me?" he asked.

She stood there holding his shoulders.

"No," she said, laughing.

"Oh, so you just wanted to touch me," he teased.

Emily felt her face grow red as she blushed.

"No, I was trying to dunk you," she admitted, quickly letting her hands slide off his shoulders, but he took a step forwards and slid his arm around her waist, his face growing serious.

Her heart lurched and nerves blossomed in her stomach. What was he doing? He looked down at her, water sparkling on his skin. They were so close. Neither of them spoke. Emily became less aware of the flowing stream and everything else around her as his eyes bored into hers, their intensity consuming. Her mind was filled only with him, not ifs or buts or consequences as her hands crept back up his arms and twined around the back of his neck. Her senses were filled with him, the dusky evening air that surrounded them, sweet apples, the familiar scent of the countryside. His skin. As he lowered his head slowly towards her the pull was so strong it was dizzying. His breath was on her lips and Emily felt her body go numb. She was certain she would have fallen over if he had not been gripping her waist like he was. Emily gazed up at the perfect Cupid's bow of his lips knowing any second that they would touch hers, for every second they didn't it was like time had stopped.

Finally Rome covered the inch between them and laid the most perfect gentle kiss on her mouth. His lips were wet from the stream, and she felt the softness of them. His hands rose up and she felt them in her hair.

She felt the release of so many unspoken words as he stole the breath from her body. They grew closer as he pulled her in and neither of them seemed to consider the consequences as their lips pressed against each other's and they began to kiss with more urgency. She felt him groan against her mouth and she knew this was the most perfect moment of her whole life until he pulled away all too soon. She stared at him breathlessly. He looked back at her. His eyes were blazing. They were wide and dark, almost wild.

"I'm so sorry," he said. For a second he looked like he might say something more but then he turned and walked up the rocks, out of the stream, leaving her standing alone, wordless. She tried to speak, but her mind was whirling. She could still feel the sensation of his kiss on her lips, the press of his stubble. The way his fingers had pressed into her skin as he'd held her. She watched as he struggled to pull his jeans back onto his wet legs. He threw his top on and turned to look at her.

"Come on, let's go inside," he said. She climbed out of the stream and got back into her shorts and T shirt. He didn't look at her as he turned to walk back up the valley towards the farm. She followed him with no idea of what she should say or do.

Rome

Rome opened the door to the house so hard that it banged against the wall as it flew open. He was furious with himself. What was he thinking? He heard Emily come in behind him and he flipped the kettle on. He felt her hovering nearby.

"I'm so sorry, Emily," he said again.

"*I'm* sorry. I shouldn't have let it happen. I should have pulled away," she replied. He took two mugs down.

"This doesn't change anything," he said, turning to face her. She nodded.

"I won't say anything," she said.

He trusted that she wouldn't. Neither of them spoke for a while. The only sounds were the birds in the garden and the dogs shuffling around on the lounge rug.

"I think I should probably go," she said.

"That's fine, we don't have to talk about it."

"No, I mean leave the farm. Move to my mum's."

Rome felt as though his heart had stopped completely. "You don't have to leave Emily, nothing has to change."

"You must know how much I care about you. I can't watch you marry Georgina. This was only temporary, anyway. Seth's leg has been better for weeks," she said.

Rome didn't know what to say. His heart ached for her.

"I want you to stay," he said, growing anxious. He watched a tear slide down her face. She brushed it away.

"I take it Georgina is going to move in with you when you're married Rome," she said. "I can't live here; it's not right. Especially now that we've kissed."

What could he say? She was right. He couldn't live with both of them and if he wanted to save the farm he had to live with Georgina. For the first time since Helen died he wondered if the farm was worth it. Would Seth forgive him if he just gave it up?

"I don't know what to say, Emily." He stood still and watched her, not knowing what would happen next. Scared to find out.

"I'll pack my stuff tonight and I'll get a cab in the morning," Emily said. "Thank you for everything. I've had the best time of my life here."

Rome felt his eyes burn as pain bloomed in his chest.

When he didn't reply she turned and walked through the living room and he heard her footsteps on the stairs. The thought of hearing those familiar footsteps replaced with Georgina's was too much to bear. His head swam in confusion as he eyed the medicine cabinet above the kettle. Now more than ever he wanted the whisky. He could have a bit. Just a few sips.

Rome opened the cupboard door as the kettle finished boiling. He took the bottle from the top shelf and unscrewed the lid without hesitation. It was natural to him since the accident. He threw it back and gulped as much as he could until his chest couldn't take the burning pain anymore. He put the bottle on the side and coughed. The whisky spread through his stomach and heat filled him. He couldn't stop himself as he began to cry.

Why did the thought of losing Emily hurt so much? It was similar to the pain he felt when he knew he would never see Helen again. Dulled but similar. Could it really be that? Could it be that he could still feel that feeling after all? A cocktail of painful and confusing feelings washed over him at the obvious revelation. He knew he liked Emily a lot but it had taken losing her to realise he had fallen in love again. It *was* possible to love two people. He would always love Helen. A part of his soul was scattered in the orchard with hers. But he loved Emily too. It was something he never thought he would feel again but each day Emily was here, his pain got a little easier to live with.

What more would his life throw at him? How much more could he take before he gave up? He covered his eyes with his forearm and rested his head down against the sideboard. He felt the tingling of the whisky seep round his body. He already knew he wouldn't find the will to stop himself from finishing the bottle. Tomorrow he would marry Georgina and she would move into his and Helen's home. Emily would leave it. He would be alone again. He heard the distant memories in his head. He saw Helen in his mind's eye. He saw her bruised and bloodied body in the small, white hospital room. He saw Emily driving away and leaving him forever. He picked up the bottle and drank until it burned.

Emily

Emily found sleep impossible that night. She could see the outline of her suitcases by the door. She would have to get the rest of her things up to her mum's in a van, the same way Mark had sent it to her here a few months back. She lay staring straight ahead of her. Moonlight glowed against the far wardrobe as it slid in through a gap in the curtains.

Emily threw back her covers in frustration and sat up on the bed. How was she supposed to sleep now? She checked her phone on the night stand. It was four o'clock. She couldn't lie in bed any longer. A surprising rage filled Emily and she couldn't control it. She had worked up a sweat. Rome should not be marrying Georgina tomorrow. It was clear he had feelings for her. He had kissed her. It had been the sweetest moment of Emily's life. She simply couldn't imagine leaving here tomorrow. For months she had spent every day with Rome; some days had been bad but most had been amazing and she had grown so close to him. She couldn't begin to imagine how much she would yearn for her life here once she was gone.

 All Emily wanted now was to feel Rome again. She wanted to go to his bedroom and tell him how she felt, *show* him how she felt, but that was impossible.

A sudden need to talk to Seth came to her. There was nothing he could say or do, nothing that could change the outcome of tomorrow, but somehow she felt like she should give it one last shot. Seth would know how serious Rome was. Maybe he would know if there was even the slightest chance Emily could convince him not to go through with it.

Emily pulled on some jeans and a dark hoodie. She tossed her hair up and took her phone from the bedside table. She opened the door as quietly as possible and tiptoed out onto the landing. Emily passed Rome's door and headed quietly for the stairs, taking them slowly. She went through the large lounge and into the sitting room, then noticed the dogs weren't on the rug as she made her way towards the kitchen. She turned to look around and saw a big black shape on the sofa in the darkness. As she edged closer she saw it was Rome, asleep with his dogs. One curled against his body and the other was behind his legs. She backed away quietly, not daring to watch him sleep. She walked through the kitchen and something glinted over by the sink. She saw it was a whisky bottle. She could smell it. Had he poured it down the sink or drunk it? By the way he was asleep fully clothed on the sofa she assumed the latter. She slipped out of the kitchen and headed for the back door.

*

The yard was glowing with moonlight as Emily strode towards Seth's cottage. The night was warm and a million stars twinkled in the sky. It dawned on her at that point that she was going to wake Seth up at four in the morning. She was almost there now though. She passed the eerily quiet lambing shed and thought back to the hours she had spent in there. Emily had brought life into the world and watched it end. She had learned a lot that she would never forget.

Emily walked until she reached the cottage and held her closed fist aloft, ready to knock. After a few seconds of consideration she banged the door. She waited a few minutes and heard nothing. She tried again, harder. The knocks of her own fist made her wary of the darkness. Finally Seth answered. His hair was matted to his forehead. He was wearing boxers and a t shirt and he looked worried when he laid his eyes upon Emily.

"What's happened?" he asked, urgently.

"Nothing, nothing. It's fine. I'm so sorry to wake you up but I was wondering if we could talk," she said.

"Come in." His brows were furrowed as he stepped aside.

Emily realised that this would be one of her last conversations with Seth since she was leaving tomorrow. Emily would miss him. He was kind and reliable, sweet and funny; the kind of person you'd be grateful to call your friend. Emily stepped into the little cosy kitchen of the cottage.

"Sorry, let me run and put some trousers on. I thought you were Rome knocking on the door."

She watched him go off into another room and he came back out in a pair of jeans.

"Do you want a drink? We may as well have a cup of tea since we're both up," he offered.

"Yes please," said Emily. She took a seat at the little oak table and watched Seth busy himself with the kettle and some mugs.

"What's up? Has something happened with Rome?" he asked. She could tell he was worried.

"No, nothing. I think he's been drinking tonight but other than that, no. Actually, I just came to talk about the wedding," she said.

Seth nodded. "What's bothering you?"

"All of it. I just can't believe he's going through with it," she said.

"If you'd known Rome as long as I have I don't think you would be shocked. He can be stubborn. Once he sets his mind on something he does it."

"I think I've gathered that."

"So I'm just going to guess that you came here to brainstorm ways to stop the wedding?"

Emily paused. "I'm not one hundred percent sure why I came," she said. "I guess I was wondering if you know any way at all I could change his mind. Maybe there's another way to save the farm that doesn't involve an unhappy marriage?"

"I really don't think there's anything either of us can do," he said. "I already told him I'd live without the farm a million times. He doesn't owe anything to my family or their legacy. I told him he doesn't have to do it for me or for Helen. She would rather have him give up the farm than be unhappy."

Seth stirred the tea and clinked the teaspoon on the rim of the mug. He put both cups down on the table.

"I know he's feeling guilty. I thought it might be the guilt that would stop him if anything. Especially with Georgina being mine and Helen's cousin and everything," said Seth.

"What?" Emily spluttered. She couldn't believe what she was hearing.

"Oh. I thought Rome would have mentioned it. I thought you had both spoken about it." Seth's cheeks turned a dark shade of red.

"I guess Rome was too embarrassed to say. It's not every day you marry your dead wife's cousin so you can keep a farm," Emily said, still utterly shocked. "How are you cousins?"

"Hang on. Let me get something," Seth left the room and returned a few minutes later with a cardboard box. He moved the mugs aside and placed it on the small table. She watched as Seth opened it and dug through some papers.

"Here. This is my father, Mike Anderson, and the man stood next to him is our landlord, Andrew Dawson, who's also my uncle," He passed a photo to Emily. She saw two young men stood in front of a huge manor house: the same house she had passed the day they went to the country show.

"Why do they have different surnames then?" she asked.

"He and my father had a big falling out a long time ago," Seth explained. "They didn't speak. It was before Helen and I were born. My father moved out of the manor house and down here to the valley. He met my mother, who was raised in the village, and then they married and he took her name so he could sever his family ties to the Dawsons. We became the Andersons."

He took a sip of tea. "My mother died when we were young children and my father raised us on the farm. Helen met Rome. He came over from Ireland to work here for the summer but then he stayed with her, they were completely in love. They married and lived in the farmhouse with my father. I moved into the shepherd's cottage partly because it's closer to the sheep so it's easier in lambing season. Partly because I wanted to give them some space especially if Rome and Helen ended up starting a family and anyway, I like my own space."

He paused, and Emily guessed that the next part would be painful.

"My father got early onset dementia and he died before his time. His will read that the farm would go back into my uncle's name. We were all absolutely shocked. We still don't know why he did that, we didn't think they had spoken for years. My uncle told us that my father had left the will with him before he died, so my uncle being a bitter man charged us rent and Helen, Rome and I struggled for years to pay and make enough money from the animals and Helen's cider business." Another sip of tea punctuated the story. "She passed away and Rome took it so hard. He carried on working the farm but he had no enthusiasm. We've been all each other's had for the last three years. We got desperate and that's when he took his chances with Georgina. I don't know if Rome has told you about Georgina and her brother. They don't get along. She knows when the estate is passed onto him he will push her out. That's why she is so eager to marry Rome as well, so she has a load of land and a nice big farmhouse."

Emily nodded. "Yes, he did say that. Although I'm not sure why neither of you told me that before."

"Rome wanted to keep this a secret, he wouldn't have wanted me telling you anything at all and I had a feeling that if you knew Georgina didn't love him then you'd get your hopes up thinking it would be easier to stop the wedding," said Seth.

"I just can't believe he's really going to do it, I guess I didn't believe it would happen at first but now it's really sinking in."

"He feels horrible about doing it but it's the only way to save the farm and keep Helen's memories alive. Letting it go would destroy him, although I'm pretty sure this marriage will too," said Seth.

"So why did your uncle and father fall out?" Emily asked. "It must have been something huge for him to want to change his name."

"We asked but he never told us. He said when we were older he would explain it all. Unfortunately he got dementia. None of us even thought to check the wills. We assumed we would be secure on the farm.

Everyone knew it was ours. But then the will turned up. The farm was given to my uncle." Seth sighed. "He pretended to be gracious. He let us stay here but he charged us the earth. If he had one decent bone in his body he would have let us keep it for ourselves."

"I see," said Emily. A persistent thought began to tug at her. It was the mention of wills. Rome had said something to her about a will when they were at the county show. He hadn't been able to finish explaining himself before they were interrupted. Was that the will Seth was talking about now? "May I?" she asked, indicating the box in front of them.

"Go ahead."

She looked into the box and pulled out some photographs. There were some of Helen and Rome. They looked smitten in every photograph. There were pictures of the farm and of Seth and Helen's father and mother.

"I haven't looked through these for a while," Seth said. "I took the box from my father's room when he died. He used to like taking pictures, recording the happy memories. Especially since we had lost our mother. She used to take lots of photos when we were children and he wanted to keep it going when she was gone."

Emily watched Seth smile fondly at the photographs. She reached her hand back into the box to take out some more but all she pulled out were papers.

"Sorry, I'm digging through your papers," she said, as she handed them to Seth.

"Don't worry about it," he said, as he flicked through the papers. He paused. Emily watched his expression darken as he discarded the other papers, keeping hold of only one. He rubbed his hand over his forehead and let out an audible breath.

"What's up?" asked Emily.

"Oh nothing." He shook his head despondently, a faraway look in his eyes. Emily gazed at the paper as Seth placed it down on the table. It was crinkled and yellowed with age but the words were plenty visible.

"It's a will," Emily said. She took the paper from the table. She read it through quickly.

In the event of my death, I leave my farm to be split equally between my two children, Seth and Helen.

Emily read that section aloud. "How have you not found this before now? Why aren't you happy?" Emily rose from her seat, hope and confusion exploding within her.

"Emily, it's not what you think. I *have* found it before." Seth glanced up at her sharing none of her enthusiasm. "Rome and I found it before you arrived at the farm. We were looking through the photos. Thinking about Helen and my family, feeling sorry for ourselves. Rome found it at the bottom of the box. Before then, I hadn't been in the box since before my father died." Seth cleared his throat. "It's honestly nothing though Emily. The date is wrong. It was written ages before the will my uncle had." Seth began sifting through the photographs leaving Emily staring at the will.

"Seth, where's the other will? The one your uncle found?" said Emily. Seth looked up at her.

"Emily, I promise you, it's useless. Rome and I have thought of every possible way–"

"Just let me see it."

"Hang on then," he said, as he left the room. She heard him rummaging in the next room. He came back with another piece of paper. "This is a copy of the will my father left to my uncle. I made him print me one from the original." He checked one against the other and held them both up to Emily. "See? The date on the will from my uncle is more recent than the one from the box."

"It doesn't mean there's nothing we can do," said Emily. She took the papers from him. "Didn't you say your father died of dementia?"

"Yes, what's that got to do with anything?"

"Did your father have dementia when this will was written?" Emily asked. "If you can prove to a court that his dementia meant that he didn't know what he was doing then I think they can revoke this latest will. Look, the signatures are different, too. Would your uncle have the capacity to forge a will and get it passed?"

"It sounds like him. He'd definitely have the money to pay a dodgy solicitor off," Seth said. "Surely we're clutching at straws, though? We don't know if a court will say the earlier will stands." Seth's eyebrows rose, his mouth parting. "It won't be enough to convince

Rome not to marry her, Emily. Even if you think there's a chance. Rome already knows about this will."

"It doesn't matter how slim the chance is, Seth. If there's anything we can do we have to try. We need to know if there's a chance that this will might stand."

"How do we find out? We only have hours until the wedding tomorrow," Seth said. The expression on his face was unreadable. Doubt, but maybe a pang of hope, hidden in the light of his eyes.

"We need to get in touch with a solicitor. I know a good one in the city. We need to find out if this is real before we do anything. We need to know what to do now; how to get the one from your uncle revoked," Emily said.

"How long will it take to get to the city?" Seth asked.

"Three hours there. Three back. If we leave now we could be there by seven. We can go to Ray's house, get him to look at it, and then leave. I guess if we're only there for an hour then we can be back by eleven," Emily said.

"They would already be at the wedding," said Seth.

"It's our only choice. Rome won't listen to us without proof," said Emily.

He nodded. "We need to go."

"We can take my BMW, it's at the end of the track. It'll be quicker."

They took the will and Seth grabbed two packs of biscuits. Emily raised an eyebrow.

"You'll thank me later," he said, as they headed out the door.

Rome

Rome woke to find himself wedged deeply in the sofa. He felt the weight of his dogs pressing against him. There were a few sweet seconds of bliss before he remembered today was the day of the wedding. His wedding to Georgina. He stretched and his dogs jumped down as he rose up off the sofa. He went to the kettle to make a coffee. His head was fuzzy from the whisky he had drunk the night before. When would Emily be down? He wasn't sure how he could face saying goodbye. Why had he kissed her? He checked the clock over by the larder to see that it was almost six. He would have to get a move on if he wanted to stick to Georgina's schedule.

Rome went out onto the farmyard with his dogs. He barely noticed the weather or anything else for that matter as he went about the morning jobs. Everything was clouded with nerves and a sickening anticipation. He finished the jobs in record time. The cattle and sheep had been out in the valley for a while now so all he had to do was fly round and check them. There was plenty of grass out in the valley this summer so they didn't need any extra hay putting out.

Bramley trotted over to him while he was doing the rounds and Rome took the opportunity to check him over and run a hand down all four of his legs. He fed his dogs and checked the clock again. It was almost seven. He had time. He thought of all the other things he could be doing today instead of getting married. He could have thrown the trailer load of hay off into the barn and stacked it up. He could have cut another field and made round bales for the cattle. It wasn't meant to rain for three of four days and it would have been the perfect time to get it done.

Rome trailed upstairs to find the suit Georgina had brought over. He eyed the bag hanging on the wardrobe door. He unzipped it, revealing the black suit. It was just a suit. He just had to put it on. One step at a time.

After taking a shower Rome walked back towards his bedroom. He passed Emily's bedroom door and paused. He lifted his hand, considered knocking but then decided against it. Instead he rushed back to his room and closed the door behind him, sighing heavily. He took out the crisp white shirt from the suit bag and pulled it on. As he did up the buttons he couldn't help but feel alone. Emily was asleep in the next room. He didn't know if she would come to the wedding or if she would leave this morning. He had thought about moving back to Ireland many times. He would have to move back in with his parents as he didn't have two pennies to rub together but he didn't think they would mind. He could find another job over there and rent a place, maybe even get a mortgage. But how could he leave when Helen was here? His life was here too, his animals and his dogs; all of the stock he and Seth had sweated and bled and worked to the bone to raise. Seth was here. He and Rome had become like brothers. Rome had put all of his money into the farm. He didn't have any siblings back home. Rome knew he would still feel lonely even when Georgina was in his bed.

He put on the uncomfortable trousers and jacket then he slipped the tie round his neck and fiddled with it for a long time. He never had to wear ties. When they went to her father's funeral Helen had tied it. When he had gone to hers Seth had tied it. Today couldn't be as hard as Helen's funeral. If he could do that then he could do this. He gave up on the tie. He would just have to swallow his pride and ask someone else to do it for him later.

Rome stood in front of the mirror. There was no one to tell him that he looked handsome. He spied the picture of him and Helen in the orchard on their wedding day, her soft blond hair falling down her back. She was cradled in his arms. The thing that scared him most was forgetting her. He wanted always to remember the feel of her in his arms, the exact texture of her skin, hair and lips. Her smell. What he would do to bury his face in her neck and breathe in her scent. He opened a trinket box on the dressing table and took out a little glass bottle. It held her perfume. He lifted the bottle to his nose and sniffed it. The nostalgia was immense. His chest instantly burned with an intense longing. He sprayed a tiny amount of the soft scent onto his collar. That way she could be there with him today. She could know that when he stood at the altar and said the vows he didn't mean them. It was her he loved. She was his angel. He touched the spot on his chest where Helen's ring lay against his heart and he told himself he could do it as his eyes brimmed with tears.

Rome gave his dogs two bones from the larder and stroked them on the head. He cracked the doors to the conservatory open so they could go out when they needed to.

"Be good," he told them.

Fifteen minutes later Rome reached the black gates of the big house and the reality became more intense. There was no going back once he went through them. No running away to Ireland and the safety of his parents. No running back to his farm, back to the orchard. It *wasn't* his farm, though. It wouldn't be unless he did this.

The gates opened electronically as Rome approached them. He pulled forwards and his tires crunched on the gravel as he drove towards the house. As he reached the end of the ridiculously long drive, lined with freshly painted white post and rail fencing, he arrived in front of the house. The courtyard was gravelled. In the centre was an elaborate water fountain which plumed into a stone pool. The circular courtyard led off two ways. One led into the gardens, although a hedgerow blocked them from view. A pergola tangled with wisteria plants offered a doorway into them, and they continued all the way around the big house. To the other side was a shingled area where he dumped his Landrover. He made his way to the front of the house which loomed tall in front of him. It was stark, bare and grey. Although some would consider it luxurious Rome just found it ostentatious. He knocked on the large wooden door. A footman dressed in tails answered.

"Mr Buckley, sir. Please come through. Georgina is expecting you presently." Did people still talk like that? The man ushered him through. The entry way was huge. The ceiling was high looking up to the banisters lining the second level. Two wide staircases flanked the side of the room, spiralling upwards. Rome had only been inside the manor a handful of times before.

He followed the footman through to a huge room where it was clear the ceremony would be taking place. Two huge wooden doors led them inside. Windows lined the side of the room from ceiling to floor. The view looked out on the wide expanse of gardens. White chairs sat in rows, forming an aisle which was overflowing with white lilies. Their smell was overpowering. The altar was at the back of the room. Behind it was a stained glass window. Georgina stepped out of a door at the far side, followed by a woman and two more footman.

"I told you the white carpet needs to be laid down the aisle. We don't have long, come on people." Her voice shrilled at the helpers who scurried off supposedly in search of a carpet. She spotted him across the room.

"Rome, you're finally here. Why are you already in your suit? I need you to help with the tables outside. You're going to get all sweaty." She marched towards him and took his hand, leading him out of the ceremony room and through to a larger one. "Rome that's a weird aftershave you're wearing. Didn't you get the one I sent you for today?" She didn't wait for a reply as she rushed ahead of him through the room. The ceiling was high and domed at the top. The dome was filled with glass panels. Flowers were everywhere. Everything was white. The tables were draped in white silk cloths.

At the far side of the ball room the French doors were wide open. They led out onto the freshly mowed lawn. More wooden tables were being put in place outside on the large patio. The lake was to the right and on the island was a pergola with white tulle draping from it and yet more lilies. There were wooden boats by the bank all decorated and ready to carry guests around the lake. The gardens stretched far down and sloped a little. There were extravagant trees and flower beds, stone statues and water features. Rome found it all quite pretentious. He never would have chosen something like this. Georgina must have had a dozen people working on this for days.

"Rome, are you paying attention to me? I said, don't worry about the benches because I don't want you getting all scruffy," she said.

"Okay. Remind me why I'm already here when the wedding doesn't start until eleven," he said.

"There's lots more to do, Rome," she said, as she marched off.

Emily

Emily and Seth had been driving over the speed limit all the way to the outskirts of London. Emily's fear of driving seemed to have miraculously dissolved as she and Seth hurtled down the motorway. The only thing on her mind was Rome and saving Bramblewood Farm. Maybe all she'd needed to calm her anxiety was a distraction.

They made it there in just over three hours. It was strange to be back there after so many months. They had parked in the carpark outside Ray's building. Emily hoped he wouldn't find it too absurd, them bursting in so early, filled with questions, when he probably hadn't even eaten breakfast yet. She had met Ray through Mark, the same way she had met everyone else since living in the city. He was a nice guy though. She, him and Mark and a few others had gone out on the occasion for drinks. She was hoping he would give her the time of day at least, despite her and Mark splitting. She was almost certain Mark would have made up some sort of lie as to why they broke up and it wouldn't have been in her favour.

"Ready?" she asked Seth.

"I guess so."

Emily buzzed number ten, the penthouse. A voice spoke through the buzzer.

"Hello?" A tinny voice sounded through the machine.

"Hello Ray. It's Emily here. Emily Rogers."

"Mark's ex?"

"That's the one," she said, sighing inwardly. She resented being known just as 'Mark's ex'. A buzzing noise sounded and the door clicked as it unlocked. Emily pushed the door and she and Seth walked into the building. It was nice, modern, but somehow Emily had come to dislike the look since being on the farm. She much preferred the tatty old farmhouse. It felt like a real home.

Neither of them spoke as they climbed into the lift and pressed the button for the top floor. It brought them up outside the door of number ten. Emily rang the bell and Ray answered. He was dressed in a crisp white shirt and tailored black trousers. He was tall and fair haired, a big hit with the ladies when they all used to go out.

"Hello Emily. Looking lovely as ever." He leant forward and kissed her on both cheeks.

"Hi Ray. Thanks for letting us up. This is Seth," she said, indicating him as he stood awkwardly behind her. The two men shook hands.

"Hi," said Seth.

"Nice to meet you. Come in." He nodded his head in the direction of the flat and Emily and Seth removed their shoes as they walked up the plush cream carpeted stairs. They reached the top where the penthouse split off in two directions. One led towards the bedrooms, Emily assumed, and the other to a kitchen which she could just see to the left of them. The walls where white and curved. Ray led them straight ahead into a living room. Leather sofas stood on a hardwood floor. The ceiling was taller than three men put together. There were glass panelled windows letting in light above them. The whole wall ahead was glass with a view that looked out over the city. It was a view Emily would have been jealous of had she not become recently accustomed to the view of the sloping hills and moorland of Devon.

"It's a gorgeous place," said Emily.

"Thank you. I like it. Why don't you both have a seat? I'll get us some drinks. What will you have?" he asked.

"I'd love a cup of tea actually. Thank you," said Emily.

"Coffee would be great, thanks a lot," said Seth. Emily could sense his anticipation. She knew he had a million questions he wanted to spring upon the solicitor.

Ray returned shortly with the drinks and he handed them out. He took a seat over by the window in a leather arm chair with an ankle crossed over one leg.

"To what do I owe the pleasure of this unexpected visit?" he asked.

"We really need some advice actually. I'm sorry to drop in so early but it's urgent. I should have called first," said Emily.

"Don't worry about it. I'm always up at the crack of dawn. What can I help you with?"

"It's quite a story actually."

"You know I've heard them all already Emily. Hit me with it," he said, smiling.

"Seth here lives on a farm a few hours out of the city. His father, Mike, died years back of early dementia and the farm they live on was passed to his uncle, Andrew Dawson, due to the wishes which were outlined in the will. Andrew lives on the estate which is attached to the farm."

"Okay," Ray said, inviting Emily to tell him more.

"There was confusion as his uncle and father supposedly hadn't spoken for years due to a family falling out. Mike even took Seth's mothers surname when they married to cut ties with the family, so, as you can imagine, they were confused when Mike left the family farm to Andrew. Mike had moved out of the manor house after the fight and moved down to the farm, which by all shouts had belonged to the Andersons ever since."

"It's possible for people to fall out and still leave things to one another," Ray pointed out.

Emily nodded. "Except there's another will. Seth found it a while back but he didn't think it meant anything. As soon as I saw it we drove straight here. The will states that the farm will go to Seth and Helen. Helen is Seth's sister who sadly passed away a few years back. They lost their mother as children. I ended up moving to this farm for some crazy reasons I won't bore you with. Seth's brother-in-law Rome also lives there. He was married to Helen. In a few hours' time he is about to marry Georgina Dawson, Seth's cousin. By marrying her he will get to keep the farm which he and Seth are deeply attached to. Their only choice is to do this because Andrew Dawson is charging them extortionate rent to stay living on the farm. Georgina has her own reasons for marrying Rome but we won't get into that. If this will we found has grounds to stand then we can drive back to Devon and stop Rome from marrying Georgina."

Emily took a deep breath, cleared her throat. She had watched Ray's eyebrows climb higher and higher until they disappeared into his hairline.

"I must say I didn't expect that. It's certainly a complicated one. Do you have the will?"

"Yes, I have it here," said Seth. He put his coffee down on the table beside him and pulled it out from his hoody pocket. He walked over to hand it to Ray.

"Thank you." Ray unfolded the will and looked it over. Emily waited in agonising anticipation as Ray's trained eyes scoured the will front to back.

"It looks real. It has everything a will needs. Witnesses, signatures. However, it also comes down to the dates. Is there any chance you know the date of the will which was used to award your uncle ownership of the farm?" Ray said.

"Oh sorry, yes, I have that too. I've got a photocopy. I made my uncle give it to me when my Father died." Seth handed the copy to Ray.

"How is it your uncle came to have the will, do you know?" Ray asked.

"He said that my father gave it to him before he died," Seth replied. Emily could tell he was nervous. The apartment wasn't his scene at all. Maybe he was just anxiously awaiting the verdict, the same as her.

"And Emily mentioned your father died due to dementia, is that correct?" asked Ray.

"Yes."

"Interesting," said Ray, as he compared the two wills at eye level. Emily and Seth glanced at each other.

"The one you discovered is dated earlier, so if both were genuine then the farm would belong to your uncle. However, there is something strange in that the signature on the most recent will is clearly different to the one you have found. It looks like they are written by completely different hands. However, I'm not an expert on that. How long did your father suffer of dementia before he died?" asked Ray.

"About four years," said Seth.

"I don't know exactly when your father died but I am guessing you would be able to line up the dates and confirm he did in fact have dementia when this most recent will was drawn up."

Seth nodded. "Yes."

"Don't get too excited. These things are very complicated and I certainly can't promise you you'll get your farm back, but, this will from your uncle seems like it could be fake. If you have had the earlier will in your possession for all this time then I'm assuming your uncle would not have had access to it. So this is your father's signature," said Ray, indicating the swirly scribble on the earlier will.

"The recent will has a different one and you say it came from your uncle. I'm wondering if he forged it. It's not uncommon. Here's the icing on the cake. If you can prove your father had dementia and was not in a fit state of mental health to make a will at the time written here then the will does not stand. The earlier will does. This would mean the farm is yours," Ray said.

Emily's heart beat fast and her palms sweated. She dared to let herself hope. She looked over at Seth. His eyes were wide as he perched on the edge of his seat. His lips parted as he stared at Ray in disbelief.

"What are the chances of us winning? I'm assuming it will be a court case," said Emily.

"It must go through the probate registry. The original district registry which the first one went to. An application must be put in to revoke the old will and put the new one in place. It will go to court and it could be expensive," said Ray.

"Rome and I have no money," Seth said. "We've given everything we possibly can in rent."

"And we only have a few hours until the wedding," said Emily. She was feeling desperate and defeated.

"There's one other thing I can suggest to you. It's not exactly by the book," said Ray.

"Go on," urged Seth.

Ray spoke for a while and Emily and Seth listened eagerly. Seth nodded.

"Do you think it will work?" Seth asked.

"I'm afraid I don't know your uncle but it's the only way you'll be able to stop it in time if Rome is as sure about marrying her as you say. Applications and court proceedings take a long time. This way you could really save yourselves some money as well. Maybe even make yourselves a little bit," said Ray. Seth nodded. He rose from his seat.

"We've got a wedding to stop. Or at least try to," he said. Emily's head whirled as she stood up. Would they be able to pull it off?

Ray walked them downstairs to the door.

"I can't thank you enough for your help," Seth said to Ray.

"Not a problem my friend, if the plan goes ahead then I can drive over tomorrow to draw up a contract." Ray replied, shaking Seth's hand.

"Thank you, Ray," said Emily, as she gave him a quick hug.

"Don't mention it," Ray leant in closer to Emily. "Also for the record. I don't believe Mark. I know how to spot a liar."

"Don't believe him? What's he said?" asked Emily.

"That you cheated on him," Ray shrugged.

"Of course he did," Emily said. "It's a total lie. *He* was the one who cheated."

Don't worry about it, that's Mark all over," said Ray.

"It certainly is," said Emily, shaking her head. "Look, thanks for everything again and sorry to rush off."

They got in the lift and hurried back to the car.

*

Emily and Seth hurtled down the motorway. That was when they saw the sign.

Accident ahead.

The traffic was built up. They slowed until they came to a standstill. It was gridlocked.

Seth cursed as he propped his elbow on the window and put his head in his hand. "What the hell do we do now?"

"Call Rome quick." Emily grabbed her phone and pulled up Rome's number. She pressed call and put it on speaker. Emily's heart quickened at each ring. It rang out.

"He never answers his bloody phone. I feel so utterly stupid not getting the will checked earlier. Now we're going to run out of time," said Seth.

Emily passed the phone to Seth. "Keep trying."

The traffic inched on and Emily let out a deep breath as she threw herself back into her seat and banged the steering wheel.

"We'll get there in time. We have to."

"Accidents can take ages to clear. It could be a pile up," said Emily. Anxiety prickled in her stomach as she pictured the crash.

"I know stopping this wedding means more to you than just helping me and Rome out, Emily," said Seth.

"What do you mean?"

"I saw you both down in the stream yesterday. I was walking across the yard." Seth gave Emily a sideways glance. "I saw you two kiss." He looked over and quickly away, his attention focused on the car ahead. "Sorry, I don't mean to embarrass you."

"No, it's fine. You're right." Emily flicked her gaze over to Seth and then out of the window. "I do have feelings for him." She shuffled uncomfortably in her seat. "I never expected it to happen and it's not the only reason I want to stop the wedding. I want to do it for you and Rome and for the farm. For Helen too."

"Well, I think he likes you back."

Emily's heart skipped. "Why do you think that?"

As he spoke Seth continued to call Rome's phone. Rome continued not to pick up.

"It's obvious. I've not seen him happy around anybody since Helen. Plus you kissed; that was my main tip off."

"I don't think he's ready to see anybody," said Emily. "He is clearly grieving for Helen."

"I'm sure he will always love and miss Helen. I know I do, every day. It doesn't mean he won't fall in love again."

"Does it upset you though? That I like Rome but he was married to your sister? Do you hate me for it?" she said.

"Absolutely not. I don't expect Rome to stay grieving for my sister for the rest of his life. I know how much he loved her. If he fell in love again I'd be happy for him," Seth grinned at Emily. "And for you," he added.

Emily smiled at him. The phone rang out again. Seth opened the glove box and took out a packet of biscuits as they inched down the road.

"I don't think he's picking up," he said.

Rome

Rome lifted a shaking hand and pressed the flute of champagne to his lips. He threw it back. It was almost eleven. Time for him to go and stand at the altar. All of the guests had arrived for the ceremony. He had watched them file in, wearing their fancy clothes. They had filled the white chairs ready to watch him chain himself to Georgina for the rest of their lives. A wave of nausea passed over him. He clutched a nearby marble pillar. A woman rushed up behind him: one of Georgina's little worker bees.

"It's time to go in, Mr Buckley," the woman said. He barely heard her as his head swam. She took his arm and forcefully guided him to the big open doors. She pushed him through and closed them behind him. He was trapped. He looked in front of him. His stomach clenched with fear. He put one foot forward and then the other. It didn't feel like him walking up the aisle. He felt disconnected. His body was doing it for him but he wasn't there.

Thousands of eyes pierced his back, side and front. He felt like a mouse walking through a den of cats. The pressure closed in on him from all around as he walked up the never-ending aisle. He reached the top after what felt like an eternity. Georgina's mother Isobelle and Brother Daniel were sat in the front row directing disapproving glances at Rome. The vicar was standing there waiting. He greeted Rome. Rome wasn't even sure if he replied. Rome looked to his right. Where was Seth? Seth was supposed to be here next to him. He was the best man. Rome felt his pocket. The rings were there. He was already supposed to have given them to Seth. He hadn't come. Rome scanned the sea of pretentiously dressed observers in their silly hats. Emily wasn't there either. He ached to see her in the crowd. The only two people who cared for him had deserted him. He felt his chest tighten. Emily was gone. He took his phone discreetly from his pocked and flipped up the screen.

There were lots of missed calls from Emily. Had something happened? Panic gripped him. He shot his eyes towards the wooden doors; the escape route. He should run. He needed to find Emily. Music started playing. The wooden doors opened. The space was filled with a wall of pink frills as a line of bridesmaids walked towards him. They filed up the aisle and stood to the left. The gleaming white of Georgina's wedding dress grabbed his attention. The sea of heads turned to gawk at her. It was too late to run. He watched Georgina walk towards him with a smile plastered on her face. Andrew had his arm linked around hers. With every step she took towards him his heart beat faster. He felt sweat dampen his back as he desperately tried to force himself to breathe. She reached him. Andrew gave her to him. She took Rome's hands. He was aware they were shaking in hers. He forced himself to look at her. Everything was happening so fast.

"Where's Seth?" Georgina said, under her breath, tilting towards him. All Rome could manage was a shrug. Then the vicar started speaking.

"Dear friends and family. We are gathered here today to celebrate the union of Georgina Isobelle Dawson and Rome Thomas Buckley."

There was nothing he could do now. It was happening. It felt so different to how he had planned it in his head. He told himself he would arrive, say the vows and get it over with. Living through it was so much harder. He started to wish he had told his parents about the wedding. At least he would have had someone in the crowd to look at and focus on. They had loved Helen and he didn't want to tell them he was already remarrying. He certainly didn't want to admit he was doing it for his own selfish needs. He didn't love Georgina. The feeling of their hands clasped together made him want to tear off his skin.

Eventually the vicar asked if there were any who had a reason why they shouldn't marry. Half of Rome prayed for someone to stand up and shout out a reason loudly. The other half knew he was doing this to save Bramblewood Farm.

Emily

Emily drove at ridiculous speeds along the Devon coast line and into Addleton. They raced towards Addleton Manor, speeding around bends and under canopies of oaks until they reached the black gates. Waiting for the electric gates to open was agony. Emily beat her hands against the steering wheel.

"Come on!" she shouted. They opened far enough to get through and she stamped down on the accelerator. They tore down the gravel path and skidded as they braked outside the water fountain in the courtyard.

"It's massive," said Emily, as they got out of the car and left it abandoned by the fountain.

"How do we do this?" asked Seth.

"What do you mean?" Emily replied.

"Do we just run out in front of everyone?"

"That's how they do it in the movies," she said. "We have to go now. We might already be too late."

They jogged towards the house. A footman at the door stopped them.

"How can I help you?" he asked, stepping in front of them.

"We have an urgent message for the groom," said Emily.

"I'm afraid I can't let you enter; the ceremony is in progress," said the footman, standing straight with his hands behind his back. Seth and Emily looked at each other.

"You can't stop us," she said. She darted behind him and opened the door. She looked behind her as Seth grabbed the footman and pushed him aside. The man shouted after them as they charged into the big house. Too many doors and rooms. Where were they?

"Which way?" Emily shouted.

"This way." She followed Seth as they ran at full speed through the house towards two wooden doors.

Rome

Rome held Georgina's hand in his shaking, sweating palm. He felt the weight of Helen's ring around his neck. His stomach twisted in a sickening sensation. The vicar pushed on.

"Do you, Georgina Isobelle Dawson, take this man to be your husband, to have and to hold from this day forward, for better or for worse, for richer, for poorer, in sickness and in health, to love and to cherish; from this day forward until death do you part?"

"I do," said Georgina.

It was his turn. It was almost complete. Time froze. He didn't feel like he was making a commitment of love; he felt like he had been shoved up on a stage stark naked in front of hundreds of people all watching and judging him.

"Do you Rome Thomas Buckley take this woman to be your wife, to have and to hold from this day forward, for better or for worse, for richer, for poorer, in sickness and in health, to love and to cherish; from this day forward until death do you part?"

Every eye in the room was on him. They were waiting for his inevitable answer. He raised his left hand to his chest. He touched Helens ring through his damp shirt. Would he be sick? The pain was physical as he forced the words out.

"I–"

Emily

Emily overtook Seth and launched herself at the doors. Heads whirled to stare at her. She saw Rome standing at the altar. Was she in time? A collective gasp resonated around the room and then there was complete silence. She didn't know what she had been expecting but this was intense. She looked behind her for Seth's support. He took her arm and they walked up the aisle. Georgina's face was twisted into vehement rage. Rome's jaw gaped and he let Georgina's hand slip from his. They reached the altar. Rome gawked at them, disbelief clear on his face.

"What is the meaning of this?" a deep voice boomed.

Emily saw a man stand up from the front row. She recognised him as Andrew Dawson. He looked just like he had in the picture of himself and Mike Anderson, which Emily had seen last night at Seth's cottage. He was just older and greyer now.

"We need to talk to Rome right away," said Seth.

"Seth, what are you doing?" Rome's voice shook. He raked a hand through his hair.

"It absolutely can't wait," said Seth.

"This is ridiculous," Andrew snapped. "You are ruining my daughter's wedding. Leave now or I'll have security remove you. Don't cause a scene."

"We need to speak to Rome privately," insisted Seth.

"Either explain yourself now or get the hell out," said Andrew.

Emily locked eyes with Rome. His expression was unreadable: confusion, disbelief, fear.

"Daddy, what's going on?" squeaked Georgina. She was ignored.

"I strongly suggest you give us a moment with Rome," said Seth.

"You can say what you need to say right this second or you will be forcibly removed," said Andrew. Emily looked at Seth. She watched his expression change and solidify.

"The will you supposedly obtained from my father is a fake," Seth announced. "The signature is forged. It does not stand because my father was suffering mentally when it was written. I have recently come across his true will. The farm belongs to me and Rome."

Emily heard the satisfaction in his voice, and she watched Andrew's face turn deep red. His eyes bulged and he resembled a whistling kettle boiling with anger.

"That's enough," he said. "You'd better come with me and we will discuss this in private."

Andrew stormed down the aisle, towards the doors.

"Andrew, what's going on?" Isobelle rushed from the front after her husband. Her face was scarlet with embarrassment.

"Come on," Seth said to Rome. He stepped down from the altar with a blank expression. They all

~ 277 ~

walked past the shocked faces, towards the exit. The sound of Georgina's heels clicked after them.

"What's this about?" she demanded.

Emily caught the tail end of hushed whispers and voices as they exited, leaving the ceremony room and the stunned guests. They followed Andrew upstairs into a large room. It was lined with leather bound books. A dark mahogany desk was at the far end. Behind it was a large window overlooking the vast gardens. The room filled with people: Andrew first, followed by Seth, Rome and Emily and lastly Georgina. Andrew turned to face them.

"Georgina, get out. This has nothing to do with you," he said.

"Daddy–"

"Now!" he cut her off. Another woman rushed up to the door of the study. It was Isobelle, Georgina's mother. Emily recognised her from the county show.

"Come on, darling," said Isobelle. Georgina burst into tears and flapped her hands as her mother escorted her from the room. Andrew walked over to his desk and leant against it. He lit a cigar, taking his time.

"Seth. My nephew. Such harsh accusations," he said.

"We're not family," Seth spat. He took the wills from his pocket.

"Don't try to deny it, Andrew," said Emily.

"What's she got to do with any of this? She shouldn't be here," said Andrew.

"Leave her alone; she has every right. It's thanks to her that I've managed to discover your betrayal of my family," said Seth. He approached Andrew.

Rome was silent. He was awaiting the scene to unfold before him.

Seth held out both wills in front of Andrew. "This is the will you forged. This is the real one." Seth indicated both in turn. "The will you made is dated when my father had dementia so even if you could convince a court that it wasn't a forgery it won't stand. I have doctor's letters to prove my father's illness. The earlier will states that the farm goes to me and my sister, just as it should be. If we take you to court you'll be punished for the forgery. I'm not exactly sure how badly but I think you have an idea. I'm sure you don't want to take the risk. They don't look highly on forgery."

Seth waited for Andrew's reply.

"What do you want?" he said, dragging on his cigar.

"We're going to settle this out of court. It's going to save us all time and hassle. I know you don't want to do prison time, Andrew. You're going to sign the farm over to us. We have a solicitor who is going to be present for that. He has kindly agreed to draw us up the documents for a small fee, which you are going to pay. You are also going to reimburse us for every penny we have paid you in rent since our father's death."

Emily couldn't believe the words coming from Seth. He was so confident. She hadn't known he had it in him. She glanced at Rome, whose mouth was wide open. Seth wasn't done.

"You're also going to throw in ten grand for compensation. We've really struggled these past few years."

Emily stifled a shocked laugh. Andrew's face was red and angry.

"What the hell makes you think I'll agree to these ludicrous demands?" he said, grabbing the corner of his desk.

"I'll happily go to court and settle it there if you'd rather. I'd love to see what they'll do to a rich, posh guy like you in prison," said Seth.

"And you?" Andrew turned to Rome. You don't love my daughter, do you?"

Rome uttered the first words Emily had heard since they burst into the wedding ceremony.

"If it makes it easier she doesn't love me either. She knows your son is going to run the estate when you die. She wants the farm and all its land."

Andrew was silent. He looked out ahead of him. He took another long drag of his cigar. Emily watched the muscles in his face twitch.

"I'll sign it over," he said, through gritted teeth. Emily felt her heart burst with joy. She watched as Seth turned and smiled at Rome. There were tears in his eyes. Rome was fighting back emotions too. Seth went to him and the two men embraced tightly, patting each other on the back. They drew apart and Seth faced Andrew.

"Just to let you know, Andrew, Emily has all of this recorded on her phone just in case you try to worm your way out. We'll be seeing you very shortly, along with our solicitor." Seth smiled and the three of them left the room.

Rome

"Oh my God," breathed Rome, as they ran down the stairs, his legs were weak and like jelly from the adrenalin. He couldn't believe it. As soon as he had seen Emily and Seth burst through the doors he knew they were there to stop the wedding. He just didn't know he could have both: the farm and his freedom.

"We'll explain it all in the car," said Seth, as they neared the back door.

"Rome," Georgina's voice called behind them. Rome spun around. She had makeup streaked down her face. For the first time he properly took in her wedding dress, hair and veil.

"Where are you going?" she said.

"I'm sorry, Georgina. We're not getting married. Your father will explain it all." Rome turned to leave.

"Rome please," she called.

"Don't pretend you love me, Georgina. Give it up. I know you're doing it for your own personal gain."

"And you weren't?" she said.

"Well, now we're both saved from marrying people we don't love. I'm genuinely sorry."

He turned to follow Seth and Emily as they ran across the gravel to Emily's car. Seth got in the back and Emily started the engine. They pulled away from the house down the gravelled drive and out onto the road.

"So, what the hell have you two been up to? I thought you'd gone Emily, and I thought you'd decided not to show, Seth."

"Emily knocked on my door at four AM this morning. She was thinking of ways to stop the wedding." Emily felt herself blush. "I took out a box of photos to show Emily pictures of my father and Andrew. We found my father's will in the box, the one we found when we were going through the box months ago. Emily insisted we take it to her solicitor friend in the city so we set off straight away and we've just got back." Seth glanced over at Emily. "Just in time to stop the wedding."

"So you've been gone all this time. And it's all true? Everything you said to Andrew?"

"Yes," replied Emily. "The will is real. The fake one won't stand. Seth explained to Ray that you don't have enough money to take Andrew to court. Ray suggested we use some light blackmail and convince Andrew to settle out of court. That way you wouldn't risk losing and you could even get a little extra back. Although I didn't know Seth would go that far."

"We deserve it," Seth insisted, with a laugh.

"We do that," said Rome. "Well done, both of you. You really saved me. Thank you."

"That's what brothers are for," said Seth. "And Emily helped a little."

Emily and Rome laughed and they rolled the windows down, turned the radio up and whooped as they drove back to Bramblewood Farm.

*

They arrived back at the farm and Emily parked her car at the top of the track.

"We're going to have to get a new car I think Emily," said Seth.

"What?"

"It seems we've come into some money and I think you need an upgrade if you're going to be staying here for good," he said.

Rome's heart leapt. In all the rush and confusion he hadn't thought about the fact that Emily might stay now.

"*Are* you going to stay?" he asked.

"It depends if you'll have me," she said.

"Of course we will," said Rome. She smiled at him. Her dimples showed and he thought she looked beautiful in that moment, even though she looked as though she'd lost a week's worth of sleep. He stopped in the track then and Emily turned towards him. He reached out to pull her into him and looked down at her face. He slid a wisp of hair behind her ear and ran his fingers down her cheek. They kissed and the tension in his body melted as she drew her hands up his back. He encircled her waist and as their lips pulled apart he buried his face into her neck and breathed her in. They parted and he held her hand tightly in his. He caught Seth smiling at them. He shot him a grin and they all set off down the track back to the farmyard.

*

"I'm going to catch up on some sleep. Ray is coming down tomorrow to draw up the contracts. We're not letting Andrew get out of this one. I just can't believe we finally got the better of him," said Seth.

"We did get one good thing out of him." Rome smiled at Emily and she blushed.

"We did that," agreed Seth. Rome hugged Seth one more time.

"Congratulations. You got your family's farm back," he said, and they pulled apart.

"It's *our* farm. I'm having the solicitor write us up as equal partners."

"You don't have to do that," said Rome, taken aback.

"I don't see it any other way. Helen and I always saw you as our equal partner," said Seth.

"I only wish she were here to see what you and Emily have managed to do," Rome said, and smiled at him.

"She'll know," Seth assured him, and turned to walk back to his cottage. This day had turned around fast.

"Shall we go for a walk?" said Rome, looking at Emily.

"Sure," said Emily. He took hold of her hand again as they walked down through the gate and out into the field.

"Let's go," he said, and they broke out into a run and hurtled down the valley. The sheep parted as they ran through the flock. Rome undid his jacket and threw it behind him letting it sail across the field. He felt like a boy again as they ran until they were out of breath. Emily laughed as he stopped in his tracks and turned to face her. He grinned as he looped his arms around her and they clung to each other tightly. He laughed and she giggled. For the first time in a long time Rome saw light at the end of the tunnel. With Emily and Seth by his side he could carry on.

They walked up the valley and the sun shone down on them. Bramley cantered over and Rome patted him on the neck. He trotted after them as they walked towards the farmyard, hand in hand.

"Rome?" said Emily.

"Yeah?"

"There's something I need to show you," she said.

"What's that?" he asked, intrigued.

"Just follow me," she said, avoiding his gaze as her fingers worried a frayed string on her jumper. Her apprehension set him on edge.

To Rome's surprise she led him to Helen's orchard. The gate stood before him. He felt his hand begin to shake. His body went cold and his palms sweated.

"Emily, I can't go in there," he said.

"I know it's Helen's orchard," she said. "I know it's where you scattered her ashes. Rome, when I first arrived I was looking round the farm and I found the orchard. I didn't even know you had lost your wife at that point. I've been in there. I'm really sorry Rome, I hope you don't mind. I did some work in there. I tidied it up."

Rome took a deep breath. He wasn't sure he could ever set foot in there again. He didn't think he had the strength. He approached the gate and placed a hand on the latch. He flicked it up and the gate fell open. Dandelion seeds blew upwards as the gate swished open. The orchard trees stood in rows, just as they always had. Plump apples weighed the branches down. The hazy summer air made it look like a picture. Rome felt a hand on his shoulder.

"I'm sorry, I shouldn't have intruded," she said.

"It looks just the same as the day we scattered her ashes," said Rome, fighting the well of emotion in his chest. "Don't be sorry Emily, I'm glad. Glad that someone is taking care of the place she loved most. This was her favourite place in the world."

He felt the emotion overflow as tears fell; happy tears for Helen, and the memories they shared. He could see them standing there now between the trees on their wedding day. Tears of relief fell for his freedom. He wasn't married to Georgina. He cried tears of joy for Seth. He was going to be able to keep the farm where he grew up, where he and his sister played in the valley and swam in the stream.

He cried tears of pain too, always pain, but he knew it would get better. One day he would think of Helen and the pain wouldn't be so fresh. Emily's hand on his shoulder comforted him and he felt lucky. He turned to face her.

"I love you, Emily." The words came naturally. He knew he did. Between all the confusion he was sure of that one fact and if it made him a bad person then so be it, but the last thing he could do was fight it. He was all out of energy.

Emily

Emily froze at the words. She looked up at his deep blue eyes, filled with tears.

"I love you too." She was surer of it than anything else.

"I'm scared, though," said Rome.

"Of what?" she asked.

"I don't want you to have to wait for me. I'm not sure if I'll ever be completely fine again. I didn't think I would ever love anybody else. I thought I'd stopped feeling."

"I'll never replace Helen, Rome, but I can be here for you. It's okay to still be grieving."

Rome threw his arms around Emily and they stood there embracing, wrapped around each other. Emily knew she would always be there for him. He might not be completely ready now, but she had patience and she could see their life together unfolding in front her. It would be filled with sweetness, love and joy. To love Rome was also to love his hurt, his sorrow and his scars; she could do that. She would be his shoulder to cry on, his friend whenever he needed it, but for now she would hold him and he would hold her in the light of the hazy summer's sun in Helen's orchard on Bramblewood Farm.

Epilogue

Summer drew to a close. The days got shorter and the trees let go of their leaves, shedding the tainted burns of the summer sun, ready to grow new and fresh next year. The view of the valley from Rome and Emily's bedroom window was coloured with bright reds, oranges and yellows. Emily, Rome and Seth brought the cattle in from the valley. The sheep would stay out a while longer until the first snow fell. Bramley was back in his stable. Rome lit the big fire in the lounge each day and the warmth radiated through the big, old farmhouse.

The day after the wedding Ray had visited the farm. He and Seth had gone over to the estate to draw up some documents with Andrew Dawson. He had been compliant. The farm belonged to the people who loved it now. Andrew had also paid back the lost rent and the ten grand Seth had requested. He had avoided a court case and Seth and Rome didn't have to worry about bills for a while. The three of them had spent the rest of the summer making hay, checking sheep and cattle and swimming in the stream. Emily and Rome had taken picnics up at the top of the valley and they had stayed out late walking until dusk. They took trips to the beach and Rome took Emily to explore Devon's coast lines. Rome still struggled some days but he was getting better. He hadn't had a drink since the wedding. He just hadn't needed it, not when Emily was with him.

Rome's parents Neave and Tom had come over from Ireland to visit at the end of summer. They had stayed for a couple of days and Emily had taken some long walks with Neave. She'd enjoyed hearing all about Rome's childhood growing up in the Irish countryside.

Emily had spent a lot of time cooking. They had eaten a lot of apple crumbles. Rome now saw them as a way to remember Helen rather than to be sad. They had big plans for next summer to reopen the brewery and keep Helen's orchard going. It would also be a good extra income for the now profitable farm.

Emily and Rome hadn't left each other's sides since the summer and neither of them planned on doing so. They would lie on the sofa each evening after spending the day grafting outdoors. They were always full with Emily's homemade dinners. Emily would lie there and listen to the crackling fire. She knew there was nowhere else she would rather be than here with Rome. He would hold her tightly knowing he had been blessed with the chance to love again.

The End

A message from Abby

Dear readers,

If you're reading this then I can't thank you enough for choosing Summer at Bramblewood Farm. It was so much fun creating my precious characters and their home, Bramblewood Farm. Rome, Emily and Seth will be back for more, along with some new characters in my next book, Snowflakes at Bramblewood Farm, which will be released before Christmas 2020.

My favourite part about sharing my writing is hearing my readers' valued opinions. I read all of my reviews and I would be so grateful if you could take the time to leave me one. I'd love to know if it made you laugh or cry or if you love the characters as much as me. Reviews help other readers to discover my work.

I love hearing from my readers so if you'd like to get in touch then please go ahead and contact me on any of the options below.

Email: abbybroomfieldauthor@hotmail.com

Instagram: @abbybroomfieldauthor

Facebook: Abby Broomfield Author

Twitter: @ASBroomfield1

All of my readers are so special to me, so, thank you!

Warmest wishes

Abby

X

Printed by Amazon Italia Logistica S.r.l.
Torrazza Piemonte (TO), Italy

16693748R00169